Auckland Colvin

John Russell Colvin

The Last Lieutenant-Governor of the North-West under the Company

Auckland Colvin

John Russell Colvin
The Last Lieutenant-Governor of the North-West under the Company

ISBN/EAN: 9783337345457

Printed in Europe, USA, Canada, Australia, Japan

Cover: Foto ©Raphael Reischuk / pixelio.de

More available books at **www.hansebooks.com**

JOHN RUSSELL COLVIN

THE LAST LIEUTENANT-GOVERNOR OF THE
NORTH-WEST UNDER THE COMPANY

BY

SIR AUCKLAND COLVIN

OXFORD
AT THE CLARENDON PRESS
M DCCCC XI

OXFORD
PRINTED AT THE CLARENDON PRESS
BY HORACE HART, M.A.
PRINTER TO THE UNIVERSITY

CONTENTS

NOTE

The orthography of proper names follows the system adopted by the Indian Government for the *Imperial Gazetteer of India*. That system, while adhering to the popular spelling of very well-known places, such as Punjab, Poona, Deccan, &c., employs in all other cases the vowels with the following uniform sounds :—

a, as in wom*a*n: *á*, as in f*a*ther: *i*, as in k*i*n: *í*, as in intr*i*gue: *o*, as in c*o*ld : *u*, as in b*u*ll : *ú*, as in r*u*le.

JOHN RUSSELL COLVIN

CHAPTER I

INTRODUCTORY

MANY may remember that glad Tuesday, the 27th
of October, 1857, when the news of the fall of Delhi
was announced in the columns of the morning papers.
'Delhi was assaulted,' ran the *Times* telegram of the
previous day from Trieste, ' on the 14th of September,
and was in possession of our troops on the 20th.'
Another line told how General Outram and Havelock report from Cawnpur, on the 19th at 6 p.m., that
the troops crossed the Ganges without opposition,
skirmishing only with advanced posts. A little lower
down was added : ' Mr. Colvin, the Lieutenant-Governor, died at Agra, on September 9.' In the outpour
of feelings overburdened during long months of sus-
pense, and in the jubilant excitement which a few
days later greeted the announcement that Outram
and Havelock had entered Lucknow, there was little
leisure to take stock of the fallen. Events were
moving fast. While Lucknow was still beleaguered,

too much remained to be achieved for more than
a passing notice of those who had succumbed. With
the return of order came questions of reconstruction.
The past, with many who had moved prominently
through it, was for a time obscured. For a few
weeks, paragraphs announcing in regretful terms the
death of the Lieutenant-Governor of Agra reappeared
in the news from India. In December, at the last
visitation of the Directors of the East India Company to their College of Haileybury, which, like
themselves, was about to be abolished, Mr. Mangles,
the Chairman, referred to him in words of conspicuous eulogy. A few days later the friendly hand
of the late Sir Charles Trevelyan recalled to his
countrymen in the columns of the *Times* the services
and the career of Mr. Colvin. His name after that
fell by degrees into temporary oblivion; to reappear,
before much time had passed, in narratives of the
events of 1857. Many, more fortunate if less prominent, who had taken part in those events, survived,
to tell in their own words, and from their own point
of view, their share in them. To others who, like
Mr. Colvin, had died in the discharge of duty, justice
was done by friends. 'I trust implicitly to you, in
case I fall,' wrote Sir Henry Lawrence to a brother,
' to see that, in the event of the loss of all my papers,
which is not improbable, my memory gets fair play.
I want no more.'

Sir Henry Lawrence in Oudh, and Mr. Colvin in
the North-West Provinces, were the officers in charge

of the two Provinces on which, in 1857, broke the
violence of the Mutinies. The one has found his
biographer; on the other, public judgment has gone
by default. His papers were dispersed. The day
had not yet come when the full tale of the events
with which he had been at one or other period of
his life identified could be told. Other questions
than those of India, other phases of Indian questions,
pressed upon attention. There grew, with the years,
round his name a legend of some want of vigour in
meeting the great crisis of 1857. In past years, and
in connexion with more distant events, he had been
charged with too great vigour. The historian of the
first Kábul war had asserted, and others had accepted
the assertion, that when he was but thirty his strength
of character, his force of will, and his powerful mind
had established over Lord Auckland, whom he served
as Private Secretary, too great an ascendency. The
same chronicler, writing later of the Indian mutinies,
found him wanting at fifty in the qualities of which
at thirty an excess had been imputed to him. The
shadow of these conflicting estimates rests upon his
grave. Happily, the last word has not yet been
said on the two great epochs with which his name is
connected. Time, which has corrected much of the
judgments, and cleared away more of the pretensions,
with which in 1842 and again in 1857 the air was
loaded, will yet allow that fair play to Mr. Colvin's
memory which, like Sir Henry Lawrence, is all that
he would have asked for. No memoir of him can

be complete in the foreground of which is not placed
a narrative of the events which, in 1837 and 1838,
brought about the first Kábul war, and a review of
some phases of the Indian Mutiny. With those incidents in Indian history these pages, therefore, must
be largely occupied.

The writer of this Memoir is very greatly indebted
to the present Lord Auckland, who has kindly placed
at his disposal the Earl of Auckland's letters and
Minutes, written while he was Governor-General, and
contained in forty-four large manuscript volumes.
Such of these papers as have been published in Blue
Books have been referred to, but their text has been
little quoted in this Memoir. Of Lord Auckland's
Indian correspondence, which contains his letters to
Sir John Cam Hobhouse when President of the Board
of Control, to successive Chairmen of the East India
Company, and to other public men, nothing has
hitherto been published. The writer has also to
acknowledge the courtesy of the authorities at the
India Office, who have permitted the publication of
certain despatches of the Secret Committee of the
East India Company, written in 1836 and 1838.
The text of these, though they have been referred
to by Lord Palmerston and Sir John Hobhouse in
Parliament, has never been printed for the public
eye. From these two sources extracts have been as
freely made as space will allow. They throw new
light on a page of Indian annals of which Kaye
has been hitherto the undisputed exponent. Of

Mr. Colvin's own papers, much perished with his library at Agra in 1857, but there remains a little of interest. During the years 1837–1839, when he was Private Secretary to Lord Auckland, he kept a diary of the work which passed through his hands. In the fourteen volumes of this diary, among notes of daily work and passages from his private reading, are preserved extracts from letters addressed to Lord Auckland or to his Private Secretary by the chief actors in the events of that time. Some of the flotsam and jetsam of his miscellaneous papers came also to the surface after the wreck of 1857. Letters of interest, written by Sir William Macnaghten when on his way to negotiate with Mahárájá Ranjít Singh the terms of the invasion of Kábul, are in the present writer's hands. So are copies of letters written by Mr. Colvin, as Lieutenant-Governor, from November 1853 to May 1857; and copies of those which he addressed to the Governor-General (Lord Canning), the Commander-in-Chief, Lord Dalhousie, and to others during the months of May, June, July, August, till within a week of his death, on September 9, 1857. The writer, finally, is much indebted to Mr. F. Reade, for allowing him to use an unpublished narrative written by his father, the late Mr. E. A. Reade, an eminent member of the Indian Civil Service, describing the course of affairs at Agra in the Mutinies of 1857.

The career of Mr. Colvin as an Indian civilian was in some respects singular. Although he was on the Bengal establishment, barely half the period of his

public life of thirty-two years was spent in Bengal.
He had found himself in Haidarábád and the Deccan
as an Assistant to the Resident at the Court of the
Nizám ; in the Upper Provinces with the Governor-
General; at Nepál as Resident; at Maulmain as head
of the Administration; in the Upper-Provinces again
as Lieutenant-Governor. His experience had been
large and varied; and except during three and a half
years' furlough from 1842 to the latter part of 1845
he had literally known no rest. Like other eminent
Indian officers of his time, it is mainly as a public
man that we must think of him. With whatever
tenderness their thoughts may have turned home-
wards—and few could have given more tender care
throughout life than Mr. Colvin to the welfare of
his children—such men saw little of their families.
Their children were brought up far away from them.
Their wives, under stress of ill-health, or similar
necessity, were frequently separated from them.
They themselves remained absorbed in affairs, and
in the varying public interests which, as they were
drawn nearer to the heart of the administration,
crowded in increasing importance round them. Nor
was there much in their Indian life to lessen the pressure of their labour. Mr. Colvin found rest in the
atmosphere of his home, the society of his friends, and
in his books. He read unceasingly; in the full hours
of his labours as Private Secretary, in the intervals
of his work on the Calcutta Bench, in the leisure of
a long furlough, in the brief moments which present

themselves to a Lieutenant-Governor. Usually he
read, pen or pencil in hand. His note books testify
to his appetite, as to the indulgence with which he
gratified it. It is as a man of affairs in public, and
as a student in private life, that in his papers and
his diaries he presents himself to us. Glimpses of
a more intimate kind may be gained when the veil
is lifted by friends (for he was a man of many
friends) who have recorded their reminiscences of
him, or by the more jealous hands of those who were
immediately connected with him.

CHAPTER II

SUMMARY OF MR. COLVIN'S CAREER

ON his father's side, Mr. Colvin was of Scotch
descent. His grandfather, Alexander Colvin, had
married at Linlithgow, in 1749, the daughter of
a clergyman in the north of Ireland, Elizabeth, known
among her people as 'bonny Lizzie' Kennedy. They
lived at Denovan, on the banks of the Carron, in
the parish of Dunipace, in Stirlingshire, where
Mr. Alexander Colvin owned large bleaching works.
According to a writer in Chambers' *Encyclopedia*,
the first bleach-field in Scotland was established by
the Fletchers at Saltoun in East Lothian about 1730.
Mr. Colvin's works were probably among the earliest
to be set up in Scotland. The art came, like Lizzie
Kennedy, from Ireland. Print-works, now in turn
removed, afterwards occupied the site of the buildings which belonged to Mr. Colvin; and of him
and his business there remains no longer any trace
on the Carron, except graves in the little kirkyard,
since stripped of its kirk, within the 'policies' of
Dunipace House. It was not in Scotland, but in
India, that the branch of the family with which we

are concerned was to spread itself. For the enter-
prising spirit inherited of their father the young men
of that branch found scope on the banks of a river
far remote from the Carron of their youth.

Among those who made their way to the Húglí,
where the path of fortune had been prepared for
them by Clive, was a son of the Denovan bleacher.
Alexander Colvin, in or about 1778, was the first of
the family to risk his fortunes in India, tempted by
what connexion, or led by what hopes, cannot now be
known. There, he established a house of business,
known later as the house of Colvin, Ainslie, and
Cowie ; and there, when in 1818 at the age of 62 he
died, his brother merchants erected to his memory
a marble monument, from the hands of Westmacott, in
St. John's, the parish church of Calcutta. They raised
also over his remains, in the South Park Street
Cemetery, a tomb on which they recorded his worth.
He had landed in India in the reign of Warren Hastings ; for Indian annals are divided, not by George
or William, but by Clive, Wellesley, Dalhousie,
their predecessors or their successors. While Hastings
was enlarging the limits of the Company's rule,
Alexander Colvin attended to his ventures. His
name not infrequently recurs in old Calcutta gazettes
and records. He may have served on a jury before
Sir Elijah Impey. He must have discussed over his
tea and his bananas the squabbles of the Governor and
his councillors ; and have presented his homage to the
adored ' Marian.' The scandal of Madame Grand

will have been to him a subject, first of discreet inquiry, and later of pious reprobation. He preferred, we may be sure, as became a sober Scotch body, the joys of his home in Hastings Street to the masquerades at Mr. Creighton's Harmonic House. In the South Park Street Cemetery, under hideous pyramids and beneath the débris of fast crumbling tombs, is gathered in its last reunion much of the vexed society which surrounded him. There is Hyde, Sir Elijah Impey's colleague; 'an honest man,' Sir Elijah thinks, 'but a great coxcomb.' There is choleric Clavering, Member of Council and Commander-in-Chief, but not the less prepared to call out his colleague, 'Curricle' Barwell, who later begged the honour of his daughter's hand[1]. There is his fellow Councillor, Colonel Monson; whose wife, Lady Anne Monson, 'a very superior whist-player,' rests with him.

Clavering and Monson had been sent with Francis from England to form Hastings' Council. No sooner had they landed on Indian soil than all three fell into a fashioned frenzy at what they termed the indignity of their reception. Soon, for two of them, a few feet of that earth would suffice. Now, not even a beggarly *Hic jacet* indicates their resting-places

[1] 'A man has followed Miss Clavering *on foot* from the East Indies; is quite mad; and scenes are daily expected, even in the drawing room,' wrote the Countess of Upper Ossory to George Selwyn in 1779. Mr. Councillor Barwell presently married Miss Sanderson, who lies also in the South Park Street Cemetery. Miss Clavering married Lord Napier of Merchistoun.

in the South Park Street Cemetery. They lie in nameless obscurity, where they held their heads so high. Generals, councillors, judges, the woman of fashion, the beauty of the hour, the man of business, the man of pleasure, rest together in that distressful acre. As we turn over the delightful pages of *Echoes from Old Calcutta*, responsive to Doctor Busteed's gentle summons the dead rise for an hour from their slumber. They renew the interrupted flirtation, exchange compliments and shots, sip at their 'loll Shrub,' pace their minuets, pull at their extinct hukkahs. Mr. Hickey is sharpening his pen and his periods in the *Bengal Gazette* office. The young bloods, with their black Cape 'Coffres' in attendance, are taking their pleasure in their pinnaces on the river, whence the strains of the French horn reach the celebrated Miss Sanderson, and the other languid ladies, as they pace in their chariots round the Lál Diggi Tank. Palankeens hurry past to Council House and Court. Mr. Councillor Francis in his budgerow hastens on the tide to Húglí, where she, *quae spiravit amores*, as he inscribes it in his Diary, is awaiting him. In the morning mist a shot is heard in the direction of Belvedere ; at the next meeting of the Council the Governor will explain to his colleagues how he has found it necessary to wing the most active of their number. The deer are dozing in Impey's Park, of which Park Street recalls the existence, and Middleton Row the main avenue. Clive's new fort thunders out its salute to the dank dawn ;

and, with the first shock to the heavy atmosphere of the Maidán, the phantoms slip back into their graves.

James, younger brother to Alexander Colvin, and twelve years junior to his brother, having been born in 1768—youngest, indeed, of eight sons—had as a lad entered the navy. Leaving it while still a midshipman, he sailed to Calcutta to join Alexander; and from the date of his arrival there, early in the eighties, until the present hour, the family has been directly represented in India, in the male line of the younger brother. James, returning later in 1789 to England to recover health, found himself present at the taking of the Bastille. In 1802 he married, in Calcutta, Maria daughter of William Jackson, 'Attorney to the East India Company,' and 'Register,' as the functionary was then termed, to the Supreme Court at Calcutta. To them in Calcutta, in the business house in Hastings Street, part of which they occupied as their own, there was born on May 29, 1807, their fourth child ; a son subsequently named John Russell, who is the subject of the present Memoir.

Like other Anglo-Indian children John Colvin was taken home at an early age. In 1812 he was received at St. Andrews, with his eldest brother Bazett, in the house of an uncle, Thomas Binny, formerly a merchant in Madras, who had married Mrs. James Colvin's eldest sister. There he remained till 1821, living for most of the time in a house now known as Prior's Gate, on the south side of South Street, immediately adjoining the Pends. The house next to it on the

west side is that 'old merchant's house,' of which
it may at one time have formed part, in which
Mr. Andrew Lang tells us that Mary Queen of Scots
sometimes lived when she sought refuge from the
politics and the pulpits of Edinburgh. Later, says
Mr. Lang, it came into the possession of Colonel
Nairne, who had been engaged in 1745 on the Hano-
verian side. In the Colonel's garden stood once a
solitary tree, known as Dr. Johnson's tree, from its
having been mentioned in Boswell's narrative. About
the year 1817, being then a bare trunk without
branches, this relic was uprooted, in the sight of
John Colvin and his younger brother, Binny.

At St. Andrews the lad attended as a day scholar
the schools of Mr. Waugh and of Mr. Moncur, each
in those days a great local dominie ; and in 1819 was
entered at the University. Mr. Waugh's schoolhouse,
which was pulled down in 1834, stood immediately
to the east of the Blackfriars' Chapel, in the present
grounds of the Madras College. The site of Mr. Moncur's school was on the ground known as Gregory's
Green (now no Green, but a space paved with cobble-
stones), at the east end of North Street, by the Fisher's
Gate. This site is now occupied by Coast Guard
barracks. In February, 1817, John Playfair being
principal, John Colvin inscribed his name in the University books. At St. Andrews he remained, as at the
other schools which he had attended, a day student;
wearing the scarlet gown, but daily tracing and retracing his steps, as he had done when he carried his

class books down South Street to the Blackfriars, or
across Gregory Green. He continued to be a student of
the University till 1821. His mathematical teacher at
the University, Robert Haldane, afterwards Principal
of St. Mary's College, when the lad was about to leave
St. Andrews, vouches under his own hand, on May 9,
1821, with much profusion of capitals, that 'during my
Experience as a Professor I have but rarely witnessed
so much strength as well as quickness of Talent, and
so much Proficiency exhibited by a Person so young.'

In 1821 he left the University, and went south to
reside with a tutor in Hampstead, who was to prepare
him for Haileybury. Mrs. Binny had died in 1813;
in 1818 Mr. Binny had left St. Andrews, and his
nephews had been transferred to the charge of a
medical man, an acquaintance of their uncle's. The
Doctor's house, known as Ketchpeel House (Ketchpeel
being, the initiated have it, a kind of tennis), still
stands in North Street, little altered but for a new
frontage and a change of tenants. The Doctor has
long since moved to a better home. The residence
at Hampstead was an experience similar to that
which many Anglo-Indian children undergo, and from
which not a few, John Colvin among them, turn in
later life with repulsion. To exchange home for a
pupil room, the love of relatives for the salaried affection of strangers, familiar surroundings and a congenial
atmosphere for the unknown, often for the dingy,
sometimes for the disreputable, is the lot of too
many Anglo-Indian children. To the St. Andrews of

his earlier years—to the kindly St. Andrews of his uncle's home—to the sea-blown links where he had mastered the mysteries of 'dormy,' of 'stimey,' of 'foursome,' of 'the honour,' to the buoyant waters of the northern sea, where he had become an expert swimmer, he returned, as will be seen, with delight, when on furlough twenty years later. But of the study at Hampstead he retained little but painful recollections. Fortunately, he had near relatives in London, whom he visited in the holidays, and who kept an occasional eye on the lad.

He entered Haileybury in 1823. Among his contemporaries were Sir Frederick Halliday, the late Sir Robert Hamilton, Sir Charles Trevelyan, Sir Henry Ricketts, and Martin Gubbins. ' I was a man of many acquaintances,' he wrote in later years, 'and somewhat gadding and social habits; all my work being done at night. You may do a good deal at Haileybury if you set yourself to it steadily,' he added; writing doubtless from his own experience. He passed out of Haileybury in 1825 at the head of his term, carrying off the honours of his year in classics and mathematics; though in Persian, a language in which he became afterwards proficient, he seems to have met with no marked success. He sailed to India in the 'Clyde' in October, 1825, reaching it on March 9, 1826. His father had left Calcutta shortly before John Colvin sailed from England. Passing rapidly through the College of Fort William, where he distinguished himself in Persian,

he was attached before the close of 1826 as an
Assistant to Mr. (later Sir William) Macnaghten, the
Registrar at that time of the Company's chief Court of
Appeal in Calcutta, with whose name his own was to
become closely associated. In the following year, on
May 10, 1827, little more than twelve months after
his arrival in India, when a few days under twenty,
he married. To his father, and probably to his
friends, it seemed too early; but life-long happiness
proved the soundness of his judgment. His wife
was Emma Sophia, a daughter of the Reverend
Wetenhall Sneyd, at that time Vicar of Newchurch,
in the Isle of Wight. When Mr. Colvin met her,
she was living with her brother, Major Henry Sneyd,
Commandant of the Governor-General's Bodyguard.
She survived her husband many years, dying in
July 1882, at the age of seventy-five; full of years,
and happy in all that should accompany old age

After serving an apprenticeship in the Bengal Province of Cuttack and in the Muhammadan State of
Haidarábád in the Deccan, Mr. Colvin found himself
again in 1830 in Calcutta, where he filled subordinate
posts in the secretariat offices, till in 1835 he was made
Secretary to the Bengal Board of Revenue. He had
meanwhile been deputed to inquire into an outbreak
of Wahábí fanaticism at Bárásat, in the neighbourhood of Calcutta; and had distinguished himself,
as a member of the Educational Committee, in the
ranks of those who under the guidance of Macaulay
were endeavouring to displace Oriental in favour of

Western instruction. In March, 1836, he was selected by Lord Auckland, on his arrival in India, to be his Private Secretary. Returning with Lord Auckland in the spring of 1842 to England, he remained there till September, 1845, when he left it for the last time. He was sent, on his return to India, to Nepál, relieving Captain (afterwards Sir Henry) Lawrence as Resident at the Court of Khátmándu. In the end of 1846 he succeeded Captain (afterwards Sir Henry) Durand as Commissioner of the Tenasserim Provinces in Burma. From thence, in the close of 1848, he was recalled to Calcutta, and took his seat on the Bench of the Company's Chief Appellate Court, where twenty-two years earlier he had begun official life as Assistant to the Registrar. On the death of Mr. Thomason he was selected by Lord Dalhousie to be the Lieutenant-Governor of the North-West Provinces. There, in the midst of his labours, the Mutinies burst on him in 1857. On September 9 of that year he closed his life in the Fort of Agra.

Mr. Colvin's career in India coincides with the later and final stages of the long course of operations which brought the Peninsula from Cape Comorin to the Indus under the flag of the East India Company. The making of British India was still, during much of his career, the chief business of the Government. The main questions of interest in public offices, in the journals, and in pamphlets and reviews, were till 1848 those of warlike enterprise, or of foreign policy. In the decade preceding his arrival the Nepál war. had placed within the Company's grasp the Himálayan provinces of Garhwál and Kumáun, and a long stretch of valuable forest at the foot of the Himálayas. Lord Hastings had put an end to the confederacy of the great Marátha States, had dispersed the Pindáris, and had secured the peace of Central India. The Tenasserim Province, Arakan, and Assam had been acquired by the Company; Bhartpur, hitherto believed invincible, had fallen. The Sikh kingdom in the Punjab, the Amirs of Sind, and the Court of Oudh were in 1826 the chief representatives of native rule in Northern and Western India. Before Mr. Colvin died, he saw Lahore, Haidarábád in Sind, and Lucknow annexed, and the geographical limits of India coterminous with the India of the Company. The needle of apprehension was henceforth no more subject to disturbance from storms in the Peninsula, but continued steadily to point, as in Mr. Colvin's day it had for a time pointed, to the North-West frontier and to the regions beyond it.

While Mr. Colvin saw the close of this epoch of Indian history, he was himself identified with the era which succeeded it. We can see now that with the acquisition of Oudh, in 1856, the East India Company had done its work. The Company, and the great instrument which had served it, became thenceforth impediments to progress. The Indian Empire, once formed, with boundaries approximate to those of the great empires of Russia and China, could only be represented by the Crown. The old Sepoy army, with its numbers, its prejudices, the position which it occu-

pied in native consideration, and the deference shown
to it by its masters, could not have been longer
tolerated. It was the emblem of Brahman supremacy;
as the Emperor, who was dozing his last hours away
in Delhi, was the symbol of Muhammadan dominion.
These pretensions were inconsistent with the paramount rule of a foreigner, established throughout
India. If there was to be free elbow-room and an
open field for the play of English forces, it was as
imperative that these should disappear as that the
Company should be dissolved. But in 1826 such
ideas would have been scouted. When Mr. Colvin
first entered the public service the old traditions of
the Company were still those by which the country
was administered. The press was not free. The
interloper, at the will of the authorities, might be
hustled out of the country. Government schools, outside the Presidency towns, were unknown. Instruction
in the English language was given only by mission-
aries or by the School Book Society. The native of
India was excluded from public employ, other than
that of the most subordinate kind. The procedure
of the Company's Courts, and the law administered
by them, were a terror to all but the evil-doer.
Appeals from the Company's Courts, in suits to which
European British subjects were parties, lay not to the
Company's chief Court of Appeal, but to the Supreme
Court, representing the Crown. Before Mr. Colvin
died, the Press had been freed, railways had been
opened, posts and telegraphs had been established,

the Englishman had been brought within the jurisdiction of the Company's Civil Appellate Courts.
The foundations had been securely laid of an executive
and a judicial native civil service. English education
had been vigorously introduced. The system of nomi-
nation by which he had entered India had been condemned, and the Indian Civil Service had been thrown
open to competition.

With the movement which had brought all this
to pass he had been from the first connected. He
had been always, as Macaulay put it of his brother-in-
law, the Indian civilian Trevelyan, on the side of
improvement. His sympathies were with progress and
enlightenment ; his friends were those who looked,
like himself, beyond the epoch of internal wars, beyond
the India of Wellesley, to a time which lay far ahead
of them, to the verge of which Dalhousie conducted
them, and which they were enabled by faith to foresee.
Elphinstone, Malcolm, and Metcalfe among his seniors,
Thomason and Trevelyan among contemporaries, were
men after his own heart. They were all of them
far in advance of their day; their aims and methods
were of the present hour. From Lord Amherst to
Lord Canning, though a century seems to divide their
several terms of office, is but twenty-eight years. If
1828 and 1856 are a cycle apart, and if the ideas of
1894, though they may differ in extent, are identical
in direction with those of 1856, it is largely because
of the labours of that group of the Company's servants
of whom Mr. Colvin was not the least conspicuous.

CHAPTER III

THE administration of Lord Amherst was drawing
to a close when, in 1826, Mr. Colvin landed in India.
For the moment there was peace, which it would be
Lord William Bentinck's care to preserve. Calcutta
some time before had been fluttered by an outbreak
of mutiny at Barrackpur in the ranks of the 47th
Native Infantry. But this was forgotten in delight at the fall of the great fortress of Bhartpur.
More recently, Chauringhi had been discussing the
terms of the treaty of Yandabu, which had extended
the flag to territories beyond the Bay of Bengal.
With that treaty, India entered on the last period of
peace which it was to enjoy during the first half
of the century. In the course of the first ten years of
Mr. Colvin's residence in the country, questions of
a class to which hitherto but little attention had been
paid began, for the first time, to attain some prominence. Instruction of the natives of India in the
English language, the general employment of natives
in higher and more responsible grades of administration, their adequate remuneration, schemes of retrench-

ment, the drafting of a code of criminal law, the survey
and settlement of the North-West Provinces, became
subjects of discussion. But before he could take part
in them, it was necessary for Mr. Colvin to serve
the prescribed course of apprenticeship, and to gain
some experience of the people in the interior of the
country.

For a few months, as Assistant to Mr. William
Macnaghten, he was subjected to the drudgery of
summarizing and of making *précis* of the intermin-
able Proceedings of which the record of appeal cases
in the Company's Chief Court was composed. Plead-
ings and counterpleadings, precedents and rulings,
the substance and the text of exhibits, evidence, oral
and documentary, were recited at length in these Proceedings with prolixity dear to the law elsewhere,
but precious to the Indian as his own soul. They
constituted a narrative and digest of the case from
its first inception in some pestilent bamboo brake, to
the moment when it was to be finally submitted for
the decision of the half-dozen English gentlemen who
dozed on the benches of the Company's Chief Appellate
Court. These Proceedings were inscribed on rolls;
written, like the roll of Ezekiel, within and without.
They stretched, when at full length, over yards. A
fellow labourer in that ungrateful acre, Sir Frederick
Halliday, noted, not without envy, the instinct with
which his colleague seized on material points, rejecting
at once what was irrelevant, rapidly bringing out the
issues, and grouping round each the arguments bearing

on it. From this labour, not barren only so far as
it familiarized him with the vernacular, Mr. Colvin
was released early in 1827 by orders to proceed to the
district and station of Cuttack, on the Bay of Bengal,
which with his wife he reached in February of that
year.

When Mr. Colvin commenced his active career, he
was yet in his twentieth year. At that time those
who knew him describe him as a frank-looking lad,
standing well over six feet, and conspicuously erect.
Under a quantity of fair hair lay a broad expanse
of forehead, indicative of marked capacity. Brown,
eager eyes which never failed to look you in the
face ; an expression of alert intelligence ; a mouth of
which the lines indicated great firmness, a straight
nose, a square jaw, and a well-moulded chin complete
the sketch of his features.

Throughout life he was rather grave and reserved
in demeanour, except to intimate friends. But under
the independence of his Scotch descent, and a certain
restraint of manner which guarded him from ill-con-
sidered intimacies, he concealed great warmth of heart,
and a rare capacity for friendship. Among his intimate
friends the strength of his affections, his unselfishness,
his considerate regard for others, and the loyalty of his
nature gained for him a degree of attachment which is
conceded to few. But in every society in which as time
passed he found himself, his powers of conversation and
his stores of information secured him cordial welcome.

'It is now thirty years ago,' said Mr. (afterwards

Sir Henry) Ricketts, on a public occasion at a later
date, ' that a fair, handsome young fellow, full of life
and full of ability, came and joined me as an Assistant
in Cuttack. We had boy judges in those days, as well
as boy magistrates; and he joined me' (Mr. Ricketts
was at that time Judge of Cuttack) 'as my Assistant.
I am afraid I cannot say what he learned there from
the acting Judge; but I recollect that we lived happily
together for a few months, when he left me to go as
an Assistant to Haidarábád.' The friendship thus
formed in his first district with Sir Henry Ricketts
was one which throughout life never failed his young
Assistant. To their first district, where they were sent
as lads on commencing Indian life, many, like him,
look back throughout their career with an affection
which no subsequent scene can share. There, unless
they were singularly unfortunate, they first met from
their seniors with that welcome and that generous
hospitality which is still characteristic of India. It
was then that they first tasted independence, and were
entrusted with public responsibilities. Their first experience of an Indian cold weather, and of Indian
spoit, is probably linked with the marshes, the jungles,
or the ravines of their first district. From that time
they began to study the character of the people among
whom their lives were to be passed, to gain some
insight into their points of view, to acquire sympathy
with them in their trials and struggles.

As the shadows of evening steal upon them in later
years, many turn with peculiar tenderness to the

brightness of that morning landscape. There rise around them the thick-scattered groves in which they have spent in tent-life such pleasant hours. Far off, sandy stretches lie cold in the morning mist; among silent wastes, the thread of a river winds its gleaming way. They stand by the village threshing-floor, listening to the talk of the country folk. There reaches them the sweet scent of the boiling sugar-juice, the droning of the uneasy sugar-mill, the plaintive stridency of the Persian water-wheel. Urchins, shouting from their platforms above the high crops, wage unequal war the livelong day against the mischievous parrot and the contentious crow. Infinite movement plays on the surface of the green sea of wheat. Under a dust-laden canopy, as the hours draw on, the shifting files of cattle move slowly home, in the eye of the setting sun. But with the brief twilight comes a great hush upon the country side. Among interlaced branches and the flecked shadows of their foliage, the silent moonlight sleeps on the white tent roofs. A passing breeze whispers presently of coming day; somewhere among the leaves a sigh responds to it ; Nature, with a rustle in all her plumage, awakes. With the first dawn, rosy blushes momentarily flush and fade in the pearly sky ; then, the sun leaps up in his ardour.

Few, without vital feelings of delight, recall these first impressions of Indian life. The landscape varies with the latitude. But what rarely varies is the consecration given to the landscape by youth, and the

dream in which is visioned the light that never was
nor will be.

Mr. Colvin throughout life retained fast hold of
the friends whom he made in his first district.   In
Mr. Ricketts he found the sympathy and the good
fellowship which to his final hour never failed him.
Another friend he made there was the Commissioner,
Mr. Pakenham, who a little later became Private
Secretary to Lord William Bentinck.   But Mr. Colvin
was not to remain long in Cuttack.   In the close of
1827 he was transferred to Haidarábád in the Deccan,
the capital of the Nizám's Dominions, as second Assistant to Mr. Byam Martin, who was at that time the
Company's Resident there.   It was a far cry for the
young couple from Cuttack, the journey being first
by sea to Masulipatam, and thence by palankeen to
their destination.

The affairs of Haidarábád had engaged the Government of India's close attention since 1820.   Its finances,
from causes which need not be now entered into, were
in disorder.   With a view of replacing them in equilibrium it had been agreed that the Resident should
be allowed a power of interference in the administration of the State which recalls recent experiments in
a less remote Muhammadan country.   The Resident
was instructed to 'employ his advice and influence
for the establishment of the prosperity of the Nizám's
dominions and the happiness of his subjects ; and in
that view to direct his attention to the following
topics—a salutary control over the internal adminis-

tration of the country: accurate accounts of all establishments, receipts, and expenditure ; the correction of abuses, and proper distribution of justice; the reduction of expense; the amelioration of the revenue system, including the customs and duties levied on commerce ; the improvement of resources ; the extinction of debt ; the efficiency of the troops retained, and the discharge of such as were useless.' On assuming office at Haidarábád in 1821, shortly after the issue of these instructions, Sir Charles Metcalfe had given vigorous effect to them. Among other measures he had arranged for the assessment and settlement of the land revenue for a definite term of years, with the village communities themselves, and without any intermediate agency of farmer or middleman. The sphere of this arrangement was limited to the Northern Division of Haidarábád. This was the work in which Mr. Colvin, as second Assistant to Mr. Byam Martin, found himself engaged from the close of 1827 till he returned to Calcutta in the latter half of 1830. The Resident's first Assistant, Mr. Edward Ravenshaw, who also became a life-long friend, was three years his senior. He received Mr. Colvin and his young wife on their arrival, and it was in his house that their first child, a son, was born. Mr. Byam Martin the Resident was a man devoted to books, and of extensive reading ; a man, therefore, not uncongenial to his second Assistant.

Mr. Colvin was employed chiefly in the work of assessing land revenue. The joint tenure, which is the life of the agricultural community in Northern India, had been set aside in Haidarábád. Each cultivator was separately assessed, and entered into his own distinct engagements for the discharge of his quota of land revenue. Thus the common village responsibility had been destroyed; the village headmen, who whether of election or by descent were the local representatives of each village community, had been put aside. The collecting officer had to deal, not with one or two headmen in a village, but with a host of small separate cultivators. Collections fell into arrears. The land revenues had to be reduced. In the destruction of joint responsibility, and in the diminished influence of the village headmen, Mr. Colvin believed, and convinced the Resident that he had found, the key to all difficulties. This had been searched for in the amount of the assessments, in the iniquity of native collectors, anywhere but in neglect of the organic structure of the village community. Looking below the surface, Mr. Colvin satisfied himself, and ultimately satisfied Mr. Byam Martin, that the system of joint village responsibility and the services of the headmen must be reverted to. The system in force dissolved the tie which bound the village together, so that each member was left to the insufficiency of his own resources. It relieved, on the other hand, the headmen from all responsibility for the performance of functions which, in native eyes, are inseparable from their office, and for which they continued to receive remuneration. It rendered the

interests of each cultivator distinct from, if not an-
tagonistic to the village community, as a whole. In
lieu of the common spirit of attachment, which unites
such a community to its headman, it substituted
a selfish detachment. It left in unfavourable seasons
no common resources to meet difficulties. The system
of settlement with village communities which Mr.
Colvin introduced into Haidarábád is identical with
the system adopted six years later in the North-West
Provinces, and afterwards in the Punjab.

Mr. Colvin arrived, in the course of his short experience at Haidarábád, at another important conclusion, in
which he anticipated the actual course of Settlement
administration in Upper India. 'Metcalfe,' he wrote
in 1830, a little later, 'has taken up the cudgels for the
propriety of minute inquiry and settlement in Revenue
assessments, in the most praiseworthy style. I am
not an advocate for the Government officers managing
directly and permanently with my old cronies the
cultivating ryots themselves. But that, as a pre-
liminary to any kind of management, the lands and
separate fields of a village should be measured, and
the scale of rate demandable on them be determined,
seems so obviously true, as a rule to be observed in
our own territories, where all instruments, means, and
applications are our own, that I wonder at its being
disputed. The work may be slow, but it is to be
hoped that our Empire will be long. That progress
is necessarily slow is no good reason why progress
should not be made at all.' All this, though obvious

in 1894, because it has been made the rule of practice since 1833, was in hot dispute in 1830. That the young Assistant at Haidarábád, who was still in his twenty-third year, should have obtained a firm grasp of it, is proof to what account he had turned his opportunities among his cronies, the cultivating ryots.

Before he left Haidarábád an incident occurred which must have given him no little annoyance. He had received from his chief, the Resident, Mr. Byam Martin, nothing but kindness; he was indirectly to prove the means of causing Mr. Martin's transfer from his charge. Students of Indian history know well the dismal pages devoted to discussion of the claims of Sir William Rumbold and the house of Palmer and Co. It is no part, happily, of this Memoir to recall them. They belong to a class of incident which is only too familiar to those conversant with life in the East. The adventurer who sets himself up in an Oriental state under powerful protection, who hopes to reap a rich harvest from financial dealings with it, and who finds that one needs a long spoon if one is to sup with an Eastern potentate, is as well known in Cairo and in Tunis as in Haidarábád. Some make, some mar their fortunes. Now it is the European who is ejected; now, the Oriental despot. There is Sir William Rumbold, and there is Ismáil Pásha. In the present instance, the Nizám prevailed, and the house of Palmer & Co. was discomfited. It fell, in 1830, with a great crash, bringing with it to the ground many leading firms in Calcutta. From the

dust and débris of its fall arose controversies and discussions without end. Bankruptcies, law proceedings,
claims and counter-claims, pamphlets, narratives,
charges, explanations—a whole literature grew round
the dismal subject. The personality of the Governor-
General became engaged in it. The members of the
Supreme Council were divided over it. Before it was
finally laid to rest, the Board of Control had dragged
the Court of Directors before the King's Bench to
answer to a writ of Mandamus. Little wonder, then,
if the figure of an Indian Múnshi is found at work
in the innermost maze.

The Resident's confidential Native Secretary was
accused by the trustees of Messrs. Palmer & Co. of
various acts of corruption. To examine these charges,
the Resident's two Assistants, with a third officer,
were formed into a Committee. As inquiry proceeded,
the Múnshi appealed for protection to his master.
Mr. Martin responded by dismissing from their posts
two of the prosecutors, English officers in the service
of the Nizám. This should have proved sufficient
avis aux intéressés. But, as the Indian phrase goes,
the Múnshi's *ikbál* was bad; his luck had turned.
When the Committee's finding against the Múnshi
was sent, with the record, to the Supreme Government, the Resident, inspired possibly by his underling,
combated their conclusions. But, when your *ikbál* is
bad, you may as well throw up the sponge. Whether
you are a Mughal Emperor, or a mere Múnshi, your
hour has come. The Supreme Government agreed

with the Committee, and condemned the Múnshi to dismissal. The Resident was transferred to an equivalent post elsewhere; his judgment merely, not his integrity, being in question. The officers whom he had so summarily dismissed from their employment were re-instated. Then, for reasons unconnected with the inquiry, the little group at Haidarábád was scattered. For the corpuscles which form the life-blood of British society in India are always in a state of circulation. Were it otherwise, the vitality of the whole body would perish. They are continually being pumped from the centre to the extremities, from the extremities finding their way back to the centre. While Mr. Martin went north to Delhi, Mr. Colvin returned to Calcutta : Mr. Ravenshaw travelled westward to Nágpur.

Lord William Bentinck had succeeded Lord Amherst as Governor-General. The Nizám, under whom the Northern Provinces of Haidarábád had been made over to British administration, was dead. The accession of a new Nizám gave to the successor of Lord Amherst an occasion of abandoning a system towards which neither he nor his masters were favourably disposed. The post held by Mr. Colvin was abolished; and in July, 1830, he retraced his steps by Masuli-patam to the capital, where he was to pass the next seven years of his life.

He was appointed an Assistant in the Revenue and Judicial Department, first for a few months under Holt Mackenzie, *praeclarum nomen* in Indian Land

Revenue annals, and then under his former friend
of the Sadr Court, Mr. William Macnaghten. 'I owe
my appointment to Macnaghten,' he wrote to his
friend Ravenshaw. 'I have succeeded in my main
object of securing, if fate enables me to retain it,
a useful interval of leisure before being lost in the
labour and detail of an executive appointment.'
During 1831 Mr. Colvin remained an Assistant in
the Judicial and Revenue Departments, of which the
Deputy Secretary, his immediate superior, was Mr.
James Thomason. Him Mr. Colvin was to see more
of when in the Upper Provinces in 1838 and 1839,
and eventually to succeed as Lieutenant-Governor.

In November, 1831, he found himself nominated
for the second time to conduct an inquiry. This
time it was not a Múnshi who was the culprit, but
a body of Bengal peasantry. The story illustrates
the many-sided life of India. It would be well if it
illustrated no more. Unhappily it also exposes the
carelessness of British officials; the venal character of
the native police; the despair of the villager, in vain
trying to obtain a hearing; his recklessness when he
can get no redress; finally his violence, ending in his
ruin. The episode has an interest of its own, because it
is a plant of a growth which eventually overshadowed
many a Mahommedan homestead in the adjoining
province of Behar. Though this rod was rooted out,
seeds of the same planting were carried to the mountains on our distant North-Western frontier, where
they were to become a vigorous forest. Thence thirty-

three years later would issue a host of armed men to
challenge Christian supremacy.   More lives would be
lost, fiercer conflict would be engaged, another enquiry
would be needed, before the Wahábí movement and
the Wahábí fanatics, whose outbreak in Bárásat took
Mr. Colvin there in November, 1831, could be regarded
as having been disposed of.   The fruits of the teach-
ing of Sayyid Ahmad, the apostle in India of the
Wahábí tenets of the creed of Islám, were similar in
kind in Bárásat, if not of equal abundance, to the
later harvest in Sitána.

'The preaching of Sayyid Ahmad in 1820–22,' writes
Sir William Hunter in *The Indian Musulmans*,
'passed unheeded by the British authorities.   He
traversed one Province with a retinue of devoted
disciples, converted the populace by thousands to his
doctrine, and established a regular system of ecclesiastical taxation, civil government, and apostolical
succession.   Meanwhile, our officers collected the
revenue, administered justice, and paraded our troops,
altogether unsuspicious of the great religious movement which was surging around them.   From this
unconsciousness they were in 1831 rudely awakened.'
Among the disciples of the new Apostle in Calcutta
was one known to his fellows as Títú Mian, to the
authorities as Mir Nisár Ali.   This man had begun life
as a small cultivator.   It was whispered that he had
been leader of a robber gang.   He drifted in course
of time to Calcutta, where he became a wrestler.
Thence he passed into the service of one of the large

landed proprietors, who kept each in his pay a retinue
of swashbucklers. The business of these bullies
was to break each other's heads over their masters'
disputes, whenever a boundary question or the right
to a plot of land had passed beyond the power of
argument. This occupation brought Títú Mian, who
was an expert at it, within the four walls of one
of the Company's jails. The experience seems to
have led to a distaste for engaging in other people's
quarrels. On his release he took ship to Mecca,
where salvation awaited him. For Sayyid Ahmad met
him; made him a disciple, and sent him back an
Apostle to India. He preached the Waháбí tenets to
the north and east of Calcutta. Many adhered to the
Apostle; some doubted; others made a scoff of him.
But Apostles are not to be lightly scoffed at. Títú
Mian, though now enlisted in the service of a divine
master, had not forgotten the cunning of the right
hand which had been once raised in earthly interests.
Hence the number of his followers waxed daily.
Then the landed proprietors began to hear of it.
They lifted up their eyes, and beheld Títú Mian with
a large following. Complaints reached them from
their tenants of forcible conversions and rude language. The matter seemed to them of questionable
issue to the Apostle and his followers; but, to themselves, pecuniarily promising. Each landed proprietor
adopted the method which he preferred in disposing
of these complaints; to Kishen lál Rái the more
excellent way appeared to be a tax upon Waháбí

beards. Two and a half rupees per beard was his
figure. Kishen lál Rái knew that he had no more
right to require two and a half rupees from Títú
Mian's chin, than he had the right to employ the
arm of Títú Mian in breaking heads over boundary disputes. But the Bengali landlord cared for
none of these things. Beards, among Wahábís, are
as numerous as chins; and apostles who wish to
promulgate new tenets on old lands must pay for
the privilege of disturbing the soil. That was the
point of view of Kishen lál Rái. It became in
a short space of time, after an interview with Kishen
lál Rái, the point of view also of the Hindu Inspector in charge of the Police Division. Wahábís
warmly differed from it; and contending that the
impost was not included in the Company's Regulations, proceeded to put their view before Mr. Alexander, the magistrate.

The inquiry dragged on from June 27 to September 2, precisely as it should not have been allowed
to drag. From the Magistrate, clearly, there was no
redress to be obtained. So Títú Mian and his followers marched off to Calcutta to lay their case before
Mr. Alexander's superior, the Commissioner, Mr. Barwell. The Commissioner was absent on tour. They
had to return to Bárásat, where every hair of their
chins was numbered. Then they felt that they had
exhausted all legal methods of redress, and that
nothing remained but to meditate vengeance. Un-
comfortable symptoms began to show themselves in

Bárásat. Landed proprietors and Police Inspectors were not sure that a zealot was such a mine of profit as he had seemed to them. 'From June 27, Mr. Alexander,' wrote the Court of Directors later, 'had been constantly warned by unmistakable signs of the coming storm, but failed to provide for it. On November 6 it descended on his head.

The zealots had begun to assemble in great numbers. By November 6 they had gathered. They began their operations in the time-honoured way in which the Muhammadan in India declares war against his Hindu brother. They seized and killed a cow, sprinkling the blood over the walls of a Hindu temple, and hanging up the carcass in front of that building. Then, a Brahman was killed. With the slaughter of a cow and a Brahman, vengeance had begun prosperously. The Hindus turned out to oppose Títú Mian and his host. Another Brahman was claimed by vengeance. From November 8 to 10, the word of his Lord and of Títú Mian grew mightily. Parties were especially sent out to lay hands on all Police Inspectors. Kishen lál Rái may have paid a visit to Calcutta about that time. Mr. Alexander appeared on November 15 with a few Calcutta militia and a body of police. Him, as was meet, the Waháhís speedily routed, with loss of killed and wounded; and now vengeance should have felt herself satisfied. The magistrate of the adjoining district, Krishnagar, Mr. E. D. Smith, came next day on the scene, preceded by a numerous body of police.

and bringing with him several European Indigo planters. After reconnoitring the insurgents, Mr. Smith, still preceded doubtless by his police, retreated. Three days later came troops; the rioters were attacked and defeated; Títú Mían 'and about fifty others' there and then achieved martyrdom. One of his disciples joined him a little later, slain judicially by unbelievers. The jails of Calcutta and of the surrounding districts were gorged.

Never was there a more miserable story. Yet it has many parallels. The Santál hill-men, the Deccan ryots, were victims of the same imbecility. The criminal, in such cases, is not the rioter denied redress, but the blundering legislator or the thick-headed magistrate. Mr. Colvin in his Report wrote :—

'The entire root of the mischief which has occurred is deep and cannot easily be removed. The powers possessed by Zamíndárs enable them to exercise a petty jurisdiction among their ryots, and to make petty exactions on all kinds of pretences. The corrupt character of the people and the defects of our own instruments pervert our administration of justice, and render it a matter of the greatest uncertainty whether we shall arrive at the truth or not in all cases in which men of wealth and influence will be injured by its detection. Our confined intercourse with the people, and consequent ignorance of many of their feelings and circumstances, allow false representations to be frequently imposed on us with the utmost boldness and but slight risk of discovery.'

All which, if not as true in 1894 as in 1831, still represents close approximation to the truth. The root of our difficulties still lies mainly in 'the defects of our own instruments and in our confined intercourse with the people.' The powerful landlord, the illegal cess, the venal police Inspector, are still at their work in India. Thick-headed magistrates exist. Blundering legislators are not unknown. Wild schemes are daily hatched below the surface. Forces generate in the calm atmosphere of British rule of which the authorities are absolutely unconscious. The East has an abundant storehouse of her own. West and East, coupled, not united, breed fresh forces. What direction all these will take, what is their volume or their vitality, none possibly may divine. Rash men unloose these elements; leaving it to those whose business it may be, to take the risk and the discredit of explosion.

As regards intercourse with the people we are not one whit more advanced, if indeed we are so far advanced as in 1831. Growing distrust on the one side is met by growing dislike on the other. But the corrupt character of the people and the defects of our own instruments may be corrected by a better system of education, by improved administration, by creating an adequately paid native Civil Service. Throughout the remainder of his career Mr. Colvin worked uniformly in this belief. From the hour when he left Bárásat he turned his attention unceasingly to the direction in which administrative remedies might be found for the evils of which he had witnessed the effects. He threw himself into

the cause of English education. He used all his
influence to secure a better class of native tribunals,
and to that end to improve the status of native judges.
As Lieutenant-Governor he gave his first care to the
Courts of Justice; and, when the Mutinies fell upon
him, he was engaged in a large scheme for the reform
of his provincial police. His compassion for the
ignorant impulses of the masses survived the shock
of the Mutinies. He had seen to what despair men
might be driven by the denial of redress. The importance had been brought home to him of dealing at
once with discontent, and of leaving no permissible
effort untried to detach from their leaders such as
were victims of sincere delusion. At a later date, the
endeavour to build a bridge of retreat for misguided
men brought him into sharp collision with the
supreme Government. When he addressed his Proclamation of May 25, 1857, to the followers of
Mangal Pándí, it is certain that there was present
to his mind the lesson brought home to it a quarter
of a century before by the fate of the disciples of
Títú Mian.

His inquiry completed, Mr. Colvin returned to
Calcutta, where in 1832 he succeeded Mr. Thomason
in his post of Deputy Secretary in the Revenue and
Judicial Department, and remained practising himself in the routine of a great central office. The
machinery of the Administration, with all its wheels,
pulleys, rods, and cranks, was working daily before
his eyes. To all, such a discipline is useful; but

to those who at a later date are themselves to hold
the reins of Government, it is almost indispensable. They thus familiarize themselves with the principles which underlie the conduct of affairs. They
observe their application, and become acquainted with
the views of men of experience and ability from all
parts of India. They see in what spirit public
business is habitually approached by those who have
the conduct of it; in what manner it is handled;
whereabouts they may look in affairs for the line
which separates the practicable from the preferable.
This kind of work makes of an Indian civilian a full
man and an accurate man. It is deficient only so far
as it fails to make him a ready man. State affairs,
while he is thus working out his novitiate, pass under
his eyes; characters and situations are discussed,
problems probed; the stir, the complex movement,
the march of public life in all its variety and ampli-
tude, goes on before him. But he is only a spectator
of the scenes which are being enacted. One day he
will be called upon, possibly, to sustain a principal
rôle. Then it will be well for him if he has for an
interval exchanged, at some previous period of his
career, the pen of a critic for the part of a performer.

During those years while acquiring much knowledge of affairs, Mr. Colvin strengthened his intimacy with many who became life-long friends.
Foremost amongst these was Mr. (afterwards Sir
Charles) Trevelyan; who, in his Memoir, recalls some
pleasant instances of his friend's generous self-dis-

regard; 'the warm and genial qualities of his heart,'
he says of him, 'were his crowning excellence.' In
those years, too, he first became acquainted with
Macaulay. 'The best way of seeing society here.'
writes Macaulay to his sister, 'is to have very small
parties. There is a little circle of people whose friendship I value, and in whose conversation I take pleasure:
the Chief Justice, Sir Edward Ryan, my old friend
Malkin; Cameron and Macleod, the Law Commissioners; Macnaghten among the older servants of the
Company, and Mangles, Colvin, and John Peter Grant
among the younger. These, in my opinion, are the
flower of Calcutta society, and I often ask some of
them to a quiet dinner.' One such dinner is recorded
in a page of Mr. Colvin's Diary, where he notes a
discussion on Pope's theory of the 'Ruling passion.'

On the Friday of every week, Sir George Trevelyan in his Life of his uncle tells us, a chosen few
met round Macaulay's breakfast-table to discuss the
progress which the Law Commission had made in
its labours; and each successive point which was
started opened the way to such a flood of talk,
legal, historical, political, and personal, that the
company would sit far onwards towards noon over
the empty teacups, until an uneasy sense of accumu-
lating despatch-boxes drove them, one by one, to
their respective offices. Educational questions were,
at that hour, being much discussed. There was
war *à outrance* between parties which had ranged
themselves under one or other of two banners.

There were the Orientalists, and the Occidentalists. The former believed in the emancipation of the Eastern mind by the study of Arabic, Persian, and Sanskrit ; the latter trusted only to English instruction. A Committee of Public Instruction had been charged with a report to the Government on the matter. Of this Committee Macaulay was President. Mr. Colvin was an ardent member, fighting in the ranks of those who advocated English instruction. Prinsep and Macaulay ' butted one another like two bulls,' said a critic, later. Finally Macaulay wrote a monster Minute, which carried all before it ; and on March 7, 1835, Lord William Bentinck decided in favour of the English section.

Lapse of years has placed the wisdom of that decision beyond doubt ; but with the lapse of years have arisen regrets for the neglect of Oriental tongues, and doubts among other points as to the value of the instruction given in India in the name of English education. Great strides have been made in England since 1835 in the physical sciences ; but to this study few Indian students apply themselves. Literature is more attractive as being more congenial, and more likely to gain remunerative employ. Hence, while the physical science class-rooms are neglected, the native students crowd round Professors who can present them to Rosalind in her forest of Arden, or will take them with Moses to the fair. Many think that if this kind of instruction, when conveyed to the Indian mind, is not defective, at least it leaves much to be desired. It calls out the exercise of memory, of imagination, of literary skill, rather than the faculty of reasoning. It is opposed to that discipline of exactness, by which imaginative minds are sobered. The Colleges and Universities turn out men who declaim in English with the fatal facility of those whose matter is below the standard of their manner. They have equipped themselves with the art of the orator and the trick of the journalist. But, moving on the surface of things, they come perilously near to be charlatans. Their imitative powers are a snare and a stumbling block to them ; for to speak other men's thought, in other men's tongues, they have bartered their own identity. With fellow-subjects from the West who are but slightly acquainted with them, they pass readily for true metal. But, to those who are more familiar with them, the defects of their mental character seem encouraged by their training. ' The fact is,' said the late Sir Henry Maine, in one of his addresses to the University of Calcutta, ' that the educated native mind requires hardening. That culture of the imagination, that tenderness for it which may be necessary in the West, is out of place here ; for this is a society in which, for centuries upon centuries, the imagination has run riot ; and much of the intellectual weakness, and moral evil which afflict it to this moment, may be traced to imagination having so long usurped the place of reason.' Yet, as there was division in 1835, so is there a division now. Few would propose to recall Arabic or Sanskrit to redress the balance. But, neither are all convinced that the present education is at fault ; or that there is to be found in the exact sciences a better means of correcting the weakness of the Indian mind than by rigorous training in metaphysics, or through the bracing atmosphere of English literature.

Again, the neglect of Eastern tongues has thrown a shadow of reproach on the British Government in India, and on its servants. The Government of India is master of the country in which the Vedas were first hymned, in which Háfiz and Saádi are household names, and in which some sixty millions regard the language of the Prophet of Arabia with idolatry far surpassing the veneration of English Universities for the dead tongues of ancient Europe. That a Government thus favoured should show itself so indifferent to Sanskrit, to Persian, and to Arabic research, is matter of unpleasant remark among Orientalists in Paris and in Vienna. Finally, the whole Muhammadan community finds itself gravely prejudiced by the educational decrees of the Government in its struggle, not to advance, but even to maintain itself under British rule. Before a Mussulman can turn his attention to our language, he must, by the usage of the society in which he moves, have made some progress in Persian, and have learned at least to repeat passages from the Kurán. By the time that these obligations have been disposed of, years have passed ; and when he turns his attention to Western literature, he finds himself distanced by his more lightly-equipped Hindu competitor.

The tale of Mr. Colvin's earlier years in India draws to a close. In 1835 he had been advanced to the post of Secretary of the Land Revenue Board. The late years had been pleasant. His wife had returned in 1833 from England, restored to health, after two and a half years' absence. He was surrounded by friends. His work was congenial. He had made for himself a foremost place in the junior ranks of the Civil Service. He had gained good experience. His active mind had thrown itself eagerly into all the discussions of his day. If his ' topics, even in courtship ' had not been, as Macaulay wrote of his brother-in-law Trevelyan, ' steam navigation, the education of the natives, the equalization of the sugar duties, the substitution of the Roman for the Arabic alphabet in the Oriental languages,' his mind, like his friend's, was ' full of schemes of moral and political improvement.' He was prominent among the most keen reformers; always forward on the side of all that was liberal. The hour of comparative leisure, too, such as it was, for which he had prayed the gods, had been granted him. He had made full use of it, and fortune had helped him to equip his mind by an opportunity unique in India. For his intimacy with Macaulay must have been fruitful, stimulating his love of reading, and quickening his mental vigour. To have been one in whose conversation Macaulay took pleasure may have been only on the part of that great man a more generous way of saying of an acquaintance, that he was one who took pleasure in Macaulay's conversation. But to have been in the course of his life one of those whose friendship Macaulay valued, is no small title to respect. From the pleasant breakfast parties and the little dinners of the Law Member of Council, as from intimacy with his own contemporaries, he was now to pass into more formal scenes and to breathe a colder and less genial atmosphere. With 1836 he was called on to undertake duties which necessarily drew between him and his friends an unwelcome veil of reserve. From that date till 1842 he stood in the fierce light which, beating on the central figure of the Government in India, searches out all who are grouped about it. The hour of leisure was over. The day of labour and of detail had come.

CHAPTER IV

PRIVATE SECRETARY TO LORD AUCKLAND, 1836-1838

LORD AUCKLAND arrived in Calcutta late in the evening of Friday, March 4, 1836, ' for the grounding of the *Jupiter* on a bank of mud detained me for some hours.' When he was preparing to leave England, he had asked all who were well acquainted with the rising men in India to give him lists of those whom they thought qualified to fill the post of Private Secretary. Many names appeared in one or other list, but Mr. Colvin's name appeared in all. Guided by this coincidence, and strengthened in the conclusions which he was disposed to draw from it by further inquiries on landing in India, he sent for Mr. Colvin. A brief interview satisfied him : the offer was made, and was accepted. During the ensuing six years Mr. Colvin's life was to be devoted to his chief. He threw himself into his new duties with all the vigour of his character and with the whole strength of his capacity. He had exceptional powers of sustained work ; and these he taxed to the utmost. In 1894 the post of Private Secretary is one of great labour and responsibility, requiring much tact, much method, sound judgment, an even temper, and a prudent tongue. But, compared with the office as it existed in 1836, the present duties are greatly changed in character. There is more correspondence nowadays with London; constant telegrams from all quarters must be received and replied to; a weekly mail from England must be mastered, and a mail to England must be weekly despatched. The railways flood the table with letters, and the anteroom with visitors. In 1836 telegrams and weekly mails were unknown; there were no railways, fewer posts, fewer strangers from the provinces or elsewhere. But if less time was taken up in maintaining communication with Europe, more was absorbed in matters of purely Indian administration. At present the Viceroy has a Lieutenant-Governor in Bengal to take from off his shoulders the burden of Calcutta and the government of seventy-one million of people. The patronage is transferred with the duties. The movements of every Bengal official, from the magnate in the Court of Appeal to the latest little fledgeling who has alighted from England on the Calcutta strand, have no longer to be disposed of as in 1836 in the Private Secretary's Office. The departments of the Government of India are divided now among the members of Council; and, subject in a few cases to the concurrence of the head of the Government, which is rarely withheld, each member, with the rest of his work, disposes of the claims of officials under him. Much of the patronage

which proved such a burden in former years is now
removed from the hands of authority, and has been
made the subject of rules and regulations.   Local
governments have also their share.   In 1894, the
officer who wishes to see the Viceroy may or may not
obtain an interview; in 1836 every civilian was held
to have the right to see the Governor-General, should
he desire it, once a week.   The Private Secretary is
still, as he was in former years, at the mercy of every
man with a grievance, a good story, or a friend to
provide for.   But many who would otherwise have
importuned him are now choked off by provisions of
Rules or Codes, or find their interest elsewhere.

The Private Secretary in 1836 had not yet bestowed
himself in the closet adjoining his master which he
now occupies.   With his establishment he overflowed
that gloomy basement in Government House which,
in its contrast to the halls and corridors above, recalls
the vast obscurities over which are pillared and by
which are sustained the beatitudes in the high
places of India.   In those spacious vaults Mr. Colvin
installed himself; and there, except during the years
when he was absent with his chief from Calcutta,
he was to be found early and late.   His energy was
of peculiar use to Lord Auckland, whose habits,
though laborious, had not been formed in that
Indian school of administration which, itself shrinking
from no drudgery, exacts drudgery from all who are
in authority.   The 'inconceivable grind' of Indian
official life to which an eminent Viceroy lately bore

testimony, is felt by no one more than by the
Governor-General's Private Secretary ; nor by any
Private Secretary has it been discharged with more
unfailing punctuality than by him whom Lord Auckland had selected. He was bound to Lord Auckland
by every tie which can attach, in public life, a man of
aspiring nature to the statesman who has given him
his first opportunity of distinguishing himself, and has
bestowed on him his entire confidence. Loyalty being
of the essence of his character, he identified himself
with the views, the successes, and the disappointments
of Lord Auckland with unquestioning ardour. So
completely did he do this, that the gossip of Calcutta
failed finally to distinguish between master and servant. The very excess of the Private Secretary's
pleasure at his master's triumphs, the depth of his
distress in the hour of his master's humiliation, were
regarded in some quarters as presumption amounting
to proof that the measures with which he so warmly
identified himself must have been of his own inspiring.
But Lord Auckland, better informed, retained his
confidence in Mr. Colvin to the last day of his life,
and fully returned the attachment with which he
never ceased to be regarded by his former subordinate.

Here is a picture of Lord Auckland from the friendly
hand of Charles Greville : —

' He was a man without shining qualities or showy accom-
plishments, austere and almost forbidding in his manner,
silent and reserved in society, unpretending both in public
and private life. Nevertheless he was universally popular

and his company more desired and welcome than that of many far more sprightly and brilliant men. His understanding was excellent, his temper placid, his taste and tact exquisite; his disposition, notwithstanding his apparent gravity, cheerful; and under his cold exterior there was a heart overflowing with human kindness, and with the deepest feelings of affection, charity, and benevolence. Engaged from almost his earliest youth in politics and the chances and changes of public life, he had no personal enemies and many attached friends amongst men of all parties.'

Mr. Greville adds that Lord Fitzgerald (who was President of the Board of Control in the course of 1841) 'had never been more struck by anything than by the despatches and State papers of Lord Auckland, and that he had no sort of idea he was so able a man; that he was, with the one exception of John Russell, by far the ablest man of his party[1].'

At the time of Lord Auckland's arrival in India, the country was externally at peace. During the brief interregnum, between the departure of Lord William Bentinck and the arrival of his successor, Sir Charles Metcalfe had acted as Governor-General. With the support of Macaulay he had repealed all regulations imposing restrictions on the press. Now, legislation of a less popular kind was contemplated. The Black Act was impending, and a cloud hung over Calcutta. Over Burma and Nepál there was also a cloud. In the Punjab the atmosphere was not clear; while

---

[1] 'Greville Journals,' vol. iii. p. 254.

a veil of mist, no bigger than a man's hand, floated over the distant mountain tops in Kábul. The questions of the moment were, the practical application of the decision as to English education which had been arrived at in the previous year; the progress of the work of the Law Commission in drafting a Penal Code; ways and means for providing the newly created class of native civil judges with a suitable rate of remuneration; steam communication with England; reform in the copper currency; and the perennial misgovernment of Oudh. For many months after he assumed office, the Private Secretary had to get up such of these matters as he was imperfectly acquainted with, and to coach his chief in all. Space does not admit of dealing with them; but a few brief lines are necessary as to the relation of the Government in 1836 with the several States adjoining it. Throughout Lord Auckland's administration they occupied much of his time, and he recurs to them in every page of his papers. Mr. Colvin's Diaries show how many were the hours which he passed in studying them : and few are probably aware, how in later days, in the midst of the Kábul enterprise, it seemed at one or another time inevitable that we should be forced into conflict with the Court of Ava, or be called on to repel an invasion of Gúrkhas from Khátmándu.

For the moment, however, 'the Burmese are quiet,' wrote the Governor-General to Sir John Hobhouse, 'and apparently friendly. We propose to give the

king of Ava a white elephant, which has been born
at Madras, and which should bind him to us for ever.'
'I have had some confidential correspondence with
Mr. Hodgson, our Resident in Nepál,' he adds [1]. 'The
politics of that State are greatly disturbed, and in
a manner not entirely without precedent. The king
would gladly change his minister and the minister
will not be changed.' (In April, 1835, Lord Melbourne
and the Whigs had returned to office.) 'He has now
been master of Nepál for thirty years, and will but
unwillingly subside into a good subject.' In the
Punjab, Mahárájá Ranjít Singh had been casting
covetous eyes on territories in the possession of his
neighbours, the Amirs of Sind. Within four months of
Lord Auckland's arrival, Captain Wade, the Governor-
General's agent at Ludhiána on the Sutlej, the
frontier of British territory, was instructed to tell
the Mahárájá that the Government 'could not but
view with regret and disapprobation the prosecution
of plans of unprovoked hostility, injurious to native
States with whom that Government is connected by
close ties of interest and good will.' Captain Wade
was to employ, and successfully did employ, his best
efforts in dissuading the Mahárájá from embarking
on such an enterprise as an hostile advance upon
Shikárpur. The control and navigation of the
Indus were objects to which the thoughts of Lord
William Bentinck had been turned; and before he

---

[1] Mr. Hodgson survived until the present year, a link with that
distant past.

left England Lord Auckland had been told to give his early and best attention to them. Hence the 'hands off' to the Punjab Mahárájá.

The affairs of Kábul had not been among those with which Lord William Bentinck had been called upon to deal. But he had given much thought to the frontier, and had left for his successor a Minute which indicated his anxiety. After pointing out that the state of Afghánistán presented at that time no cause of alarm to India, he turned to the growing influence of Russia over Persia. 'From the days of Peter the Great to the present time the views of Russia have been turned to the obtaining possession of that part of Central Asia which is watered by the Oxus, and joins the eastern shore of the Caspian. The latest accounts from Kábul state that they are building a fort between the Caspian and Khiva. This is their best line of operation against India, but it can only be considered at present as a very distant speculation.' On the other hand, Lord William wrote, 'the line of operation of a Russo-Persian army to advance upon Herát is short and easy.' He finds the distance from Russian territory to be 1,189 miles, which he divides into four stages. He assumes that Russia could supply Persia with an auxiliary force of 30,000 men, and 'with a good understanding between the two Governments, with time for preparation, and with good management, there could be no difficulty in transporting this force to Herát.' From that point she might proclaim a crusade against British India,

'in which she would be joined by all the warlike
restless tribes that formed the overwhelming force
of Timúr.' Again carefully calculating distances, he
points out that from Herát to Attock is a distance of
1,032 miles, which he divides into four further stages.
'The Afghán confederacy, even if cordially united,
would have no means to resist the power of Russia
and Persia. They probably would make a virtue of
necessity, and join the common cause; receiving in
reward for their co-operation the promises of all the
possessions that had been wrested from them by
Ranjít Singh, and expecting also to reap no poor
harvest from the plunder of India. But, however this
may be, it will be sufficient to assume the possibility
that a Russian force of 20,000 men fully equipped,
accompanied with a body of 100,000 horse, may reach
the shores of the Indus.' Lord William Bentinck was
far from wishing it to be understood that he thought
that such an attack was imminent, or even probable.
But he thought it possible; and the object of his
Minute was to review the resources which the
Government of India had at its command in order
to frustrate such an endeavour.

Reserving further mention of Kábul affairs, this
narrative returns to Calcutta, where war is not a
contingency, but is raging furiously. The burning
question of 1836 is Macaulay's Black Act. By this
project, appeals by European British subjects from
the decisions of the subordinate Civil Courts of the
Company are in future to be taken not to the

Supreme Court, established by Royal Charter, but to
·the Company's Chief Court of Appeal, the Sadr
Diwáni Adálat.' Against this proposal the gorge
of Calcutta rises. The press, which Macaulay had
helped a few months before to free, uses its liberty
to turn on him and rend him. The English Bar
leads the opposition. As the field of that Bar's
practice is mainly in the Supreme Court, its disin-
terestedness is not wholly above suspicion. Threats
of ·personal violence are used ; the native observes,
and will note for imitation, the sentiments with
which the columns of the Calcutta papers are
crowded. Forty-seven years later, the most discreditable of these diatribes will seem like the piping of
Meliboeus contesting with Corydon, when compared
with the torrent of abuse which will be lavished
on one of Macaulay's successors. In 1883 it will be
desired to extend the criminal jurisdiction of Native
Magistrates over European British subjects. The
sack or the sea with which Macaulay was threatened
will promise euthanasia compared to the torments
then prepared for the Legal Member. Macaulay
remained unmoved. His draft became law. On the
slopes over which had flowed the molten lava of his
adversaries' wrath, smiling spring reasserted herself.
Administration resumed its appointed course. The
indigo planter continued to buy and bargain, the
ryot to make and to break his agreement. The
Company's Chief Court of Appeal showed itself
quite competent to control either party, as every

dispassionate observer had foreseen would prove to be the case.

Lieutenant Waghorn, of the Company's Marine, has meanwhile been deputed to Egypt, to probe the question of steam communication, *viâ* the Isthmus of Suez, between India and England, of which he is the confident advocate. The long trail of smoke from the funnel of the *Hugh Lindsay* has been seen between Babelmandeb and Suez. The term 'steam mail' is finding its way into the despatches which toil over the tumbling seas by the Cape. Chinamen have been consulted as to the quality of Assam tea, and have expressed very high approval of it. It will be long, thinks the head of the Government, before the depopulated country of Assam will rival China in the production of tea, even if the first difficulties of a first experiment are surmounted. But, in its higher districts, Assam, he tells Sir John Hobhouse, is a promising and healthy Province.

So 1836 and the first half of 1837 pass. 'Macaulay has given us his Penal Code.' Madras is raising disagreeable questions about the attendance of military bands at the religious functions of Indians, which so disturb the gentle temper of the Governor-General as to cause him to underline an emphatic declaration that nothing will move him from the path of religious neutrality. The financial authorities are occupied with the issue of a revised copper currency, and with the provision of funds for meeting the increased salaries of native Civil Judges, in which latter subject the Law Member and the Private Secretary take amazing interest. The latter finds time to make long extracts in his diaries from all manner of authors, writing on every variety of subject. His modest balance at his bankers, he finds, is increasing. So, in more noticeable proportions, is his family. But he may look forward to many years of employment. On May 29, 1837, he records the completion of his thirtieth year. The future is on the knees of the gods.

In June, 1837, Lord Auckland wrote to Sir James Carnac, at that time Chairman of the Court of Directors :—

'The hot season has this year been a trying one, and we have felt it more than we did last year. My appetite for going up the country, so as to pass one summer in the hills, is growing upon me. . . . It would be useful to me personally to know the men upon whom I have most to depend; to compare modes of administration, and to see public works; and I should not defer such experience until the period of my residence here shall be drawing to a close. I think, too, that my presence may have a useful effect upon our relations on the North-West Frontier, and, possibly, upon the affairs of Oudh. It will be of advantage for me, too, that for the discussion of many subjects I shall find the Commander-in-Chief in the north.'

On June 19 a Minute was signed, embodying the arrangements to be made for carrying on the work of the Government in Calcutta, and for administering Bengal, during the Governor-General's absence from that city. The Commander-in-Chief had preceded the head of the Government, and would rejoin him

E

in the summer at Simla. The Members of Council left in Calcutta were Mr. Ross, the Vice-President (who would also govern Bengal), Mr. Macaulay, Mr. Shakespear, Mr. Robertson and Col. Morison, the military member.

Mr. Macnaghten was the Secretary selected to accompany Lord Auckland. With the Governor-General there went to the North-West Provinces, besides his Private Secretary and Mr. Macnaghten, General Casement, Secretary to the Supreme Government in its Military Department, an experienced and sagacious man, who, in 1839, became Military Member of Council, and died, Sir William Casement, in Calcutta in 1844. The Commander-in-Chief it has been said was awaiting Lord Auckland in Upper India. He was, *ex officio*, a Member of the Supreme Council. Mr. Torrens—as Deputy Secretary in all Departments with the Governor-General—and the staff of military aides de camp made up the party.

From Tuesday, October 17 to Friday, October 20, the Private Secretary will be 'engaged chiefly in arrangements for departure'; on October 21 begins that journey from Calcutta to Simla of which the incidents have happily been preserved for us by Lord Auckland's sister[1]. 'We got up at five this morning; the servants were all in a fuss; when we came down for some coffee the great hall was full of gentlemen who had come to accompany his lordship to the Ghát. Even Macaulay turned out

---

[1] '*Up the Country*'; by the Honourable Emily Eden.

for it.' The coffee is hastily swallowed, compliments
and good wishes are exchanged, a procession forms
up and moves on, dignified and bright with uniforms
where the Governor-General and his colleagues lead
it, but a little ragged and playful in the rear. The
band plays a march in the 'Puritani.' The troops
who line the road on either side present arms.
A great particoloured crowd looks on. The guns
fire, the gentlemen wave their hats, the Governor-
General walks down between the soldiers ('not so shy
as he used to be at these ceremonies,' thinks his sister),
returning the long salute. Arrived at the Ghát he
makes his last adieux, gives his arm to Miss Eden, and
steps on to his barge. 'There was a great deal of
martial show,' writes her younger sister, the Honourable Frances Eden, in an unpublished Diary, 'and
guns doing their salutes ; we stepping gracefully on
board, " clad in paradoxical emotion," the suit in which
the immortal author of Santo Sebastiano always
clothed his heroes.' The curtain thus falls on Lord
Auckland's first term of residence in Calcutta. When
next he walks in procession to the Ghát it will be to
embark for England. Before then much will have
happened. But at six in the morning of this twenty-
first day of October, 1837, nothing of that is visible in
the morning mists of the capital. So the spectators
wave their handkerchiefs, and turn back to resume
their gallop round the racecourse or hurry home to
their early tea and toast, while the little group of
travellers floats down the Húglí.

The party reached Benares at ten on the morning of Tuesday, November 14, landed at five in the evening, and 'drove four miles through immense crowds and much dust' to the ground where their camp was awaiting them. From that day began the splendour of a Governor-General's progress, drawn for us by Miss Eden's graphic pen; 'the journey that was picturesque in its motley processions, in its splendid crowds, and in its barbaric gold and pearl.' Public display, Miss Eden was to find, means often private discomfort; but she regretfully foresees the day, now dawned, when 'the Governor-General will dwindle down into a first class passenger with a handbag.' The long procession moves before us as in a mirror: from that first Tuesday evening when 'everybody kept saying, "What a magnificent camp," and I thought I had never seen such squalid, melancholy discomfort,' to the last evening of Saturday, March 31, when, at Pinjaur, at the foot of the Himálayas, 'we gave a farewell dinner.' We escort the Governor-General to his tent,' which he cannot endure.' The bugle sounds at half-past five to wake us, and we are off at six, as the clock strikes. As we canter along in the mist, Giles, his lordship's valet, comes bounding by; 'in fact, run away with.' Rosina, Miss Eden's Muhammadan Ayah, *du haut de son éléphant* saláms to us. The poodle Chance's black nose peeps out from under the shawl of the liveried varlet who is carrying him. The big man as he alights cracks his little jokes; the aides de camp 'are in a roar of laughter for half an hour.' St. Cloup, the *chef*, is cursing and clattering among the country cooking-pots. Guns are incessantly booming. The Rájás come and go, swaying in their gilded howdahs ; the 'irregular horsemen. like parts of a melodrama, go about curvetting and spearing.' Prince Henry of Orange joins the camp, a fair, quiet-looking boy; 'very shy and silent' he seems at first ; but is pronounced presently 'the most comparative, rascalliest, sweet young prince ; indeed, able to corrupt a saint.' At Lucknow, which we reach on December 27, the king is too ill to see us ; but his son, who has come to Cawnpur and has been received in Darbár by the Governor-General, does the honours of the Oudh capital. On Wednesday, January 3, the scene abruptly changes. Long before we left Calcutta, the effects of the failure of the rainy season in the Upper Provinces had begun to make themselves felt. Early in September the expediency of marching a large camp through the distressed districts had been discussed. But it had been decided that supplies should be procured from Oudh ; and that as the march would be on the fringe of the threatened famine, and for a few days only, the project should not be abandoned. Now on Wednesday we are entering the famine zone. 'We left Cawnpur on Tuesday, and now that we are out of reach of the District Societies, &c. the distress is perfectly dreadful. You cannot conceive the horrible sights we see, particularly children ; perfect skeletons in many cases, their bones through their skin, without a rag of clothing. and utterly

unlike human creatures.' Food is daily distributed;
sometimes 2co, sometimes 700 are fed; we get all
our supplies from Oudh, where there is no famine.
On January 13 the camp crosses the Ganges into
Rohilkhand, passing out of the famine tract, as it
must pass out of these pages.

The whole life of a Governor-General of India is in
truth a march; his term of office, one brief procession.
Viceroy after Viceroy passes with his suite. Scarcely
has one had time to look round his camping-ground
before his successor's tents are approaching. The
golden Rájás salám to them as they come, and speed
them as they leave. Brilliant horsemen curvet about
them. My lady, wreathed in smiles, is devoured by
mortal ennui. Sweet young princes arrive, shy and
silent at first, yet most comparative, rascalliest too.
The great man, alighting, jokes; the company and the
cannon roar. These all come and go. The villagers
remain, and suffer hunger. There remains too, the
great field of British administration, with its groups
of unremembered workers. They furnish the humble
labour by whose exertions every new arrival is passed
on his way. Long after each Viceroy has returned
westward to titles, to honours, to a banquetting
Mansion House, a gracious Windsor, these *adscripti
glebae* remain. After the dust, the din, and the
salutes are forgotten, they will be still found at their
ungrateful toil; at the task of breaking the stubborn
soil, sowing the seed of progress, and watching the
scanty harvest. As the night approaches, when no

man can work, they will plod to their homes in obscurity.

During the five months which elapsed between October 21 and March 31, events beyond the frontier had been from their side marching, too, to meet the coming camp. But there remain a word or two to be gleaned from Mr. Colvin's diary. At Patná, as he passed up the river, the Private Secretary had seen General Ventura, a French officer in Sikh employ, who assured him of the Mahárájá Ranjít Singh's devotion to the British, and warned him against Burnes's loquacity. At Cawnpur, Sir Charles Metcalfe, the Lieutenant-Governor of the North-West Provinces, presented himself, only to take his leave; and thenceforth, for the two ensuing years, the Governor-General of India became also the titular Lieutenant-Governor of the North-West. Other affairs of great pith and moment were to occupy Lord Auckland in 1838 and 1839; and the conduct of the North-West administration was practically left in the competent hands of its Secretary, Mr. James Thomason, Mr. Colvin's former superior. From that time its affairs pour their full stream into those channels of the Private Secretary's diary through which the business of Bengal had hitherto flowed. There crowd into its pages terms unfamiliar in the Lower Province: thirty years' settlements, coparcenary tenures, resumption of revenue-free holdings, Act IX of 1833, all the jargon familiar to the Civil Officer in Upper India. New names, too, especially

peculiar to that Province, appear. Every Province in
India has its own Anglo-Indian names, as it has its own
diseases. Boulderson, Merttins-Bird, Raikes, Montgomery recur; a glimpse or two is caught of an active
youngster, John Lawrence, who would do admirably
for the important district of Cawnpur, it is thought.
At Benares, the Private Secretary rides off to see the
great Buddhist tope at Sárnáth, guided by an aide de
camp who is afterwards to be eminent in the annals
of Indian archaeology as Sir Alexander Cunningham.
The famine is everywhere reflected in the diary, as
are the efforts made to meet it. The Emperor at Delhi
had declined to receive on equal terms the representative of the East India Company. He had therefore
not exchanged visits with Lord Auckland, but is
waited on by the three Secretaries. At Delhi, also,
under the shadow of the Mughal's palace, is found
a Christian convert, once a Brahman priest, Anand
Masáhi, pronounced in the Diary to be 'energetic
and interesting, yet not without thought of worldly
matters.' He has now a salary of 80 Rs. per
month, and finds Christian comforts pleasant, but
ecclesiastical biography questionable. 'His notion is
that there is no record of the death of St. John at
Patmos; that the Apostle is still alive, and has
appeared as the Sikh Nának.' The question in dispute
between the Company's representative and the representative of the house of Timúr came to an issue and
was disposed of on September 14, 1857. The Emperor
rose and went his way. But Brahman converts, 'not

without thought of worldly matters,' remain in Delhi to ponder Christian problems. We wrestle now not against flesh and blood, but against the rulers of the darkness of this world.

On April 7 Mr. Colvin arrived at Simla. He had left the camp at Saháranpur on March 12 to join his wife at Karnál, where four days previously a fifth son had been born to him. Lord Auckland meanwhile had marched through Dehra Dún to Mussooree; and, returning on his steps, reached Simla on April 3.

Some fuller account is now required of the relations between the Government of India and the countries beyond the Sutlej. But, before entering upon it, a few words are needed to explain why so much space is about to be devoted in this Memoir to a sketch of the events which led to the first Kábul war. In Sir John Kaye's History the responsibility of the war has been laid upon Lord Auckland's Indian advisers. As the Governor-General was absent from his Council throughout 1838, his advisers were assumed to have been the Secretaries who accompanied him. Since then, fifty-six years have passed; and documents to which Sir John Kaye made little reference, can now be quoted in their entirety. They show whose were the instructions under which Lord Auckland acted; and what were the measures indicated for his adoption. They prove that the policy of 1838 was not that of Lord Auckland's Indian subordinates, but of his English masters. It is therefore necessary in this Memoir to trace the course of their influence on the development of affairs in 1837 and 1838. This is the object of the pages immediately ensuing. Much has had to be condensed; not a little, to be omitted But nothing essential has been lost sight of; while an endeavour has been made to place in their true light transactions hitherto very imperfectly apprehended.

It needs much mental effort to take our stand in the India of 1837. Nearly forty years of peace have accustomed us to think of our rule as paramount beyond dispute in India. But in 1837 twenty years had not passed since our position had been challenged by the Maráthás. The siege of Bhartpur, only in 1826, had been looked on as a test of British supremacy. Within our frontiers our rule was in unstable equilibrium. Outside them, we were still engaged in the struggle for mastery with other powers. Nepál threatened invasion. The Sikh kingdom loomed large and formidable on our North-West frontier. Means of concentrating troops were small. Not a generation had passed since we had obtained Northern India. The people had changed masters like sheep. Yet it had ever been an unruly race, and might prove little content to be so transferred. Within, without, was insecurity. Anxiety and apprehension are magnified in such conditions. Most men in those days admitted that India might without difficulty be invaded. The threat of Napoleon was still fresh in the public mind. So cold and unimaginative a statesman as Lord William Bentinck regarded the possibility of invasion as a contingency in view of which the strength of the army of India must be even at that distant date considered. Though Persia and Russia were far off, what safety lay in mere distance? A people who had come with their armies in long months round the Cape, could not feel much security in considerations of remoteness. Our British troops were few and in the air, being nearly half a year distant from their base. Was the Cossack on the Caspian practically further?

To understand the position when Lord Auckland set foot in India, and to what point it had arrived when he alighted in Simla, review is required of events which had been passing in Persia and in Afghánistán since the early years of the century. The relations of Great Britain with Persia had long engaged attention both in Downing Street and in Calcutta. To baffle Napoleon the British Government had despatched Sir Harford Jones to Teherán; the Government of India had sent Sir John Malcolm. The mission of the latter bore no diplomatic result; but the envoy of the Cabinet succeeded, in spite of misunderstandings with the Company and its Governor-General and his Council, in effecting a treaty with Persia. It bore date March 12, 1809, and contained an agreement for mutual aid. The Sháh would allow no European force to pass through Persia towards India; if India were attacked or invaded by the Afgháns, or by another Power, Persia would furnish a force for its assistance. On her part Great Britain would

engage, should an European force invade Persia, to
assist either with troops, or a subsidy and the loan of
officers.   British officers were sent to Tcherán to drill
the Sháh's soldiery.   A second treaty was provi-
sionally signed at Tcherán on March 14, 1812, and
was definitely concluded between Great Britain and
Persia on November 25, 1814.   By this treaty the
amount of the contemplated subsidy was fixed.   The
Persian Government further bound itself to use its
influence with the States of Central Asia on behalf of
Great Britain should any force, purposing to attack
India, advance by that route.   By Article VI it was
stipulated that if Persia were at war with any
European Power while at peace with Great Britain,
the latter would endeavour to mediate.   Mediation
failing, and provided that Persia had not been in
the first instance the aggressor, Great Britain would
either send a force from India, or would pay during the
war the prescribed amount of subsidy.   Articles VIII
and IX arranged that, if the Afgháns were at war
with the British, the Sháh would aid the latter with
troops, at the cost of Great Britain, in numbers to
be settled between the two Governments.   If war
broke out between Afgháns and Persians, the British
Government would not interfere, unless its mediation
should be applied for by both.

The fear of France passed with the fall of Napoleon.
Now, apprehension of Russia arose.   In 1813 a long
period of unequal war between Russia and Persia had
been brought to a close by the Treaty of Gulistán.

'By this treaty,' says Kaye, 'Persia ceded to Russia all her acquisitions on the South of the Caucasus, and agreed to maintain no naval force on the Caspian Sea: whilst Russia entered into a vague engagement to support, in the event of a disputed succession, the claims of the heir-apparent against all competitors for the throne.' British officers remained in Persia, doing little good. Then came again war with Russia in 1826, followed by the complete defeat of the Persians, and in 1828 by the treaty of TurkmánChai. By the treaty of TurkmánChai the Caspian became a Russian lake; and two provinces were wrested from Persia. Neither men nor money had been furnished by Mr. Canning to Persia during this war, under the treaties of 1814, though both had been anxiously asked for. Teherán passed, and has remained, under the predominant influence of Russia. From that moment the countries which lie on the North-West Frontier of India again came into the foreground of the field of British and Indian politics. The risk which had led to the treaties of 1809 and 1814 reappeared; but the Power with whom we had entered into alliance to avert it was now likely to add to its imminence. For Muhammad Sháh, who, in 1834, succeeded to the throne of Persia, was understood to be wholly under Russian influence. Far from being a buckler to Great Britain against invasion of India, he was now to prove the weapon of offence. He at once renewed the project of attacking Herát, which, under the guidance of his father, the late Crown

Prince, he had entered on in 1833, but had abandoned because of his father's death. Pretext for attack was found in ancient claims of the Persian dynasty over the Herát valley; and in the seizure and sale by the Herátis of Persian subjects into slavery.

In Herát was Sháh Kamrán, an old debauchee, nephew to Sháh Shujá-ul-Mulk. This latter prince in his person (his elder brother, Sháh Zamán, being blind) now represented the Suddozái clan of the Durání tribe; and claimed the rightful occupancy of the Durání throne in Kábul. During the first decade of the century, Sháh Shujá had once failed, but had ultimately succeeded, in regaining the throne of Kábul, from which in 1801, his brother, Sháh Zamán, had been expelled. In the last year of that decade he had been again driven out; had passed through the hands of Mahárájá Ranjít Singh, leaving the Koh-i-Núr in the old Sikh's claw; had found asylum in British India; had again in the fourth decade, with the connivance of Ranjít Singh, invaded, and had been repulsed from Afghánistán. Now, discredited in the eyes of all Afgháns as a man possessed by evil fortune, a man whose '*ikbál*' was bad, he rested, with his blind brother, at Ludhiána, the British frontier station on the Sutlej, and watched events. Their nephew, Sháh Kamrán, meanwhile, was to defend Herát as best he might against the Persian King.

The Durání tribe, to which Sháh Shujá, Sháh Zamán and Sháh Kamrán belonged, comprises among its sections the Populzái and the Bárakzái. To a clan of the former, as has been said, belonged these princes : to a clan of the latter (the Bárakzái) belonged a family whose members were once their lieutenants, but within recent years had supplanted them. They were represented in Kábul by Dost Muhammad Khán; in Kandahár by his brothers, Kohun Dil Khán and others. The Bárakzái confederacy, though successful against Sháh Shujá, had difficulties of its own. The Kandahár brothers looked with greed towards Herát, and with anxiety towards Persia ; Dost Muhammad could not rest so long as Pesháwar was in Sikh hands. It had belonged to the kingdom of Afghánistán ; but had been wrested from the Bárakzáis in 1834 by the Sikhs, through the treachery of Sultan Muhammad Khán, its ruler, another of Dost Muhammad's brothers. To recover Pesháwar had been the aim of overtures from Dost Muhammad to Lord William Bentinck, and on his arrival in 1836 to Lord Auckland. These failing, he had addressed himself to Persia, had dispatched an emissary to St. Petersburg, and was now awaiting the result.

In the Punjab, the Mahárájá Ranjít Singh, surrounded by his Sikh host, was approaching his last hour. But in spite of chronic intemperance he retained complete control of affairs. He had been angered at the interdict laid by Lord Auckland on his projected enterprise in 1836 against Sind. But the old man had no wish to try conclusions with the British army. ' What the Governor-General whispers in my ear, that will I do,' was his reply to Lord

Auckland's agent. The Amírs of Sind had learned through the Governor-General's agent, Colonel Pottinger, the friendly offices of the British Government in respect of Ranjít Singh's designs. They had been told that the return which 'his lordship looks for from the Amírs for any assistance which we may render them, is that they should come fully and heartily into our plans for re-establishing the trade on the Indus.'

When in the early months of 1836 the Sirdár Dost Muhammad Khán, renewing the overtures which he had made to Lord William Bentinck, had addressed himself to Lord Auckland, on his arrival in India, he had been told that the British Government would not interfere with the affairs of independent States. In June, 1836, Mr. Ellis, the British Ambassador at Tcherán, was informed by the Political Secretary, that the Government of India would at the present moment form no military alliances with any of the countries which lie between India and Persia. In regard to them, as with all neighbouring States, Lord Auckland's wish was for peace and friendly relations. But he would see with regret and displeasure any violent or unprovoked aggression made upon their territories. At that time little was known as to the actual state of the threatened attack on Herát. The Government in Calcutta was extremely ill informed of the strength and position of parties in Afghánistán. The first point which must be arranged for was to supply this embarrassing

want. The only measure which Lord Auckland desired to push on, was the measure favoured by his
predecessor and by the Cabinet in London, the commercial opening up of the Indus. In September, 1836,
Captain Burnes received instructions to make his way
up the Indus, *viâ* Sind and Peshâwar, to Kâbul, and
to carry out a commercial treaty. He was at the
same time to acquaint himself and his masters with
the state and strength of parties in Afghánistán.

A few months after Lord Auckland had expressed
himself to the ruler of Kâbul, and to Mr. Ellis at
Teherán, in the reserved language which has been
quoted, we find him, in correspondence with Sir
Charles Metcalfe and Sir John Hobhouse, already full
of apprehensions. The 'link formed between Indian
and European politics,' the 'influence of European
politics already felt at Herât,' 'the time which, whether
we wished it, might or might not come, when we
should be obliged to exercise our influence,' 'apprehensions of our being involved at no distant date
in political and military operations upon and beyond
our frontier,'—such expressions as these are not easily
to be accounted for when we think of the assurances
given to the Amír, and the calm tone of Mr. Macnaghten's letter to Mr. Ellis.

' I share with you,' Lord Auckland wrote on September 24
to Sir Charles Metcalfe, ' in the apprehension of our being at
no distant date involved in political and possibly in military
operations upon or beyond our western frontier ; and even
since I have been here more than one event has occurred

F

which has led me to think that the period of disturbance is nearer than I either wished or expected. . . . The importance which is attached to the free navigation of the Indus, most justly I think, yet perhaps with some exaggeration, from its value not having been tried; the advance of the Persians towards Herát, and the links which may in consequence be formed between Indian and European politics, also lead me to fear that the wish which I had, to confine my administration to objects of commerce and finance, and improved institutions and domestic policy, will be far indeed from being accomplished. But, as you say, we must fulfil our destiny.'

A little later, on October 7, the Governor-General tells Sir John Hobhouse that he had written to Sir Charles Metcalfe that he would gladly avoid all interference in the politics of the West, but that the influence of European politics was already felt at Herát, that the elements of discord had long been collecting in that quarter, that the time, whether we wished it, might or might not come when we should be obliged to exercise our influence ; and that we were at least bound to maintain, if possible to strengthen our position. ' So stands the question. I think I am right, and shall be glad if I am thought so at home. But I shall be still more glad if, by the course of events, it shall be proved that it little signifies whether I am right or wrong.'

To understand these letters, we must look elsewhere than to the Húglí or the Sutlej. In Whitehall the growth of Russian influence at Teherán had become a subject of increasing anxiety. Canning had gone ; and since November, 1830. Lord Palmerston,

with but a brief interval, had been Foreign Secretary.
So far as defence against a European Power was
concerned, the Treaty of 1814 had become waste
paper. Since in 1828 Russia overshadowed Teherán,
the cover of Persia no longer existed between Europe
and India. In 1835 Mr. Ellis was sent, shortly after
Muhammad Sháh's accession to the throne of Persia, as
ambassador to Teherán. He was to warn the Persian
Government against allowing themselves to be incited
by the Russian Minister into forcing a war on the
Afgháns. Mr. Ellis, after arrival at Teherán, suggested
that danger from the West should be anticipated by
sending an envoy to Dost Muhammad Khán, and by
offering him British officers to drill his army. Meanwhile a little host of Anglo-Indian officers, foremost
among them Burnes and Conolly, had been let loose to
explore Central Asia. In the first days of 1836 it
had become finally certain that the Sháh of Persia
was meditating an attack upon Herát; and it was
known that in this object he was encouraged by
the Russian Minister. Article 9 of the Treaty of
1814 precluded Great Britain from unsolicited interference. But it is very doubtful whether the
direct interference of the English Cabinet had ever
come within Lord Palmerston's plans. If India was
threatened, by India the attack must be baffled.
The approaching crisis was not an English, but
an Indian crisis. 'This course was necessary for
the defence of our Indian possessions. I say, for the
defence of our Indian possessions, because, when we

are told that the war was undertaken with a view to European interests, I utterly deny the position. If we had no empire in India, we might have been perfectly indifferent whether Persia succeeded or did not succeed against Afghánistán. The course we pursued was entirely with a view to the security of our Indian Empire, and it was not an European but entirely an Indian question[1].' If measures could not be taken from the West to recover at Teherán the ground lost in 1828, India must look to herself for protection from attack. To that end she must secure her north-west frontier. The system of 'buffer-States' must be initiated. It was for the Indian authorities to look to their own safety, and to enter into an understanding to that end with the several States which adjoined India.

Scarcely had Lord Auckland embarked when Lord Palmerston installed at Teherán as Minister a man who might be relied upon to keep the Government of India up to the mark. In 1836 there had appeared in London a pamphlet entitled ' Progress of Russia in the East.' The pamphlet was anonymous, but it was known to have been written by Mr. M<sup>c</sup>Neill, formerly a medical officer in the Company's service.

'Few and indifferent are the regards bestowed by most European statesmen on the countries eastward of the Caspian,' wrote Mr. M<sup>c</sup>Neill, 'or even on the more known and less savage realms of Persia; yet it is there notwith-

---

[1] Debate of June 23. 1842, on Mr. Baillie's motion ; Lord Palmerston's speech.

standing that the danger to British interests is greatest and
most imminent. . . . It signifies little to object that the
Russian troops are not even yet at Herát; the time may
not be ripe for the last decided step of military occupation;
but it is fast approaching, and all is prepared to take
advantage of the proper moment; and if England remains
as indifferent to the present and the future as she has been
to the past that consummation will speedily be witnessed.
The regiment,' added the pamphlet, ' that is now stationed
at her (Russia's) farthest frontier-post on the western shore
of the Caspian, has as great a distance to march back to
Moscow as onward to Attock on the Indus, and is actually
further from St. Petersburg than from Lahore, the capital
of the Seikh. The battalions of the Russian Imperial Guard
that invaded Persia found, at the termination of the war,
that they were as near to Herát as to the banks of the Don;
that they had already accomplished half the distance from
their capital to Delhi; and that therefore, from their camp
in Persia, they had as great a distance to march back to
St. Petersburg as onward to the capital of Hindustán.
Meanwhile the *Moscow Gazette* threatens to dictate at Calcutta the next peace with England, and Russia never ceases to
urge the Persian Government to accept from it, free of all cost,
officers to discipline its troops and arms and artillery for its
soldiers, at the same time that her own battalions are ready to
march into Persia whenever the Shah, to whom their services
are freely offered, can be induced to require their assistance.'

The pamphleteer who published these words was
the Minister selected by Lord Palmerston in the year
of their publication to represent Great Britain in
Persia. If no other symptom were forthcoming of
the views which found favour in England, we should
have here very strong presumption that Lord Auck-

land was in possession of instructions pointing to
what would now be termed a forward policy. We
shall find that such in truth was the case. Now,
though Lord Auckland might succeed in attaining his
ends by diplomacy, he must face the possibility of war.
He could not be sole master of his means. This uncertainty would be reflected in his correspondence;
which we see alternately breathing hope and apprehension. That we have here the explanation of the
seeming contradiction in his language will be clearer
after perusal of the despatch bearing date June 25,
which Lord Auckland received in 1836, from the Secret
Committee of the Court of Directors. This Committee, in plain English, was Sir John Hobhouse,
who, as President of the Board of Control, had a seat
in the Cabinet. This despatch is not mentioned in
Sir John Kaye's *History of the Afghan War.* Yet
without it, the whole of Lord Auckland's policy is
unintelligible. We shall see that when finally he
decided on war with Dost Muhammad, he referred
to this despatch as the warrant for the decision to
which he had been guided.

'We have received' (wrote the Secret Committee) 'from
the Commissioners for the affairs of India, copies of two
letters which the Right Honourable Henry Ellis addressed
to Viscount Palmerston on February 25 and April 1 last—
the former stating the particulars of an overture said to have
been made by Dost Muhammad of Kábul to the Sháh of Persia
in view to the conquest and partition of the territories of
Prince Kamrán of Herát, and the latter mentioning that
a similar overture had been received by the Sháh from the

Chiefs of Kandahár, and that there was also a rumour of the Khán of Khiva having entered into an engagement with the Russian Government.

'As Mr. Ellis does not state that he has communicated with your Lordship in Council on the subject of these despatches, copies of them are enclosed for your information.

'The facts above mentioned are clearly indicative of a disposition on the part of the rival Chiefs of Afghánistán to engage the Sháh of Persia in their views of personal aggrandisement; and from the views which the Sháh himself is known to entertain in respect to Herát, there is reason to apprehend that he may be disposed to countenance any scheme which may facilitate the accomplishment of a favourite object of his ambition, encouraged as he doubtless will be by the Russians to extend his influence, and through him their own, in the countries bordering upon our Indian possessions.

'Mr. Ellis mentions, in his letter of February 25, that he suggested to Hájí Husain Alí, the Afghán nobleman from whom he received the particulars of Dost Muhammad's overtures to the Sháh of Persia, the propriety of Dost Muhammad himself opening a communication with the Governor-General of India, and it is therefore probable that before this letter reaches you, you may be in possession of an overture from this chief which will enable you the better to judge as to what steps it may be proper and desirable for you to take to watch more closely, than has hitherto been attempted, the progress of events in Afghánistán, and to counteract the progress of Russian influence in a quarter which, from its proximity to our Indian possessions, could not fail, if it were once established, to act injuriously on the system of our Indian alliances, and possibly to interfere even with the tranquillity of our own territory.

'The mode of dealing with this very important question,

whether by despatching a confidential agent to Dost Muhammad of Kábul merely to watch the progress of events, or to
enter into relations with this chief, either of a political or
merely, in the first instance, of a commercial character, we
confide to your discretion, as well as the adoption of any other
measures that may appear to you to be desirable in order to
counteract Russian influence in that quarter, should you be
satisfied from the information received from your own agents
on the frontier, or hereafter from Mr. McNeill, on his arrival
in Persia, that the time has arrived at which it would be right
for you to interfere decidedly in the affairs of Afghánistán.

'Such an interference might doubtless be requisite, either
to prevent the extension of Persian dominion in that quarter,
or to raise a timely barrier against the impending encroachments of Russian influence.

'We shall transmit to Mr. McNeill a copy of this despatch
for his information and guidance, and you may expect to
receive from him intelligence sufficiently full and accurate
to assist you in coming to a decision on the important
question to which we wish to direct your immediate and
most earnest attention.'

It is evident that Lord Auckland's position after
the receipt of this important despatch was clearly
and squarely laid down for him. First, he was to
endeavour to enter into commercial, or into political
relations with Afghánistán. He was to adopt any
other measures which he thought desirable in order
to counteract Russian influence in that quarter, if
he were satisfied that the time had arrived for
him to interfere decidedly in the affairs of Afghánistán. Such interference might doubtless be required
to prevent the extension of Persian dominion in

that direction, or to raise up a timely barrier against impending encroachments of Russia. His immediate and most earnest attention was to be given to the subject.

With this despatch in his pocket, and with Mr. McNeill never ceasing, week by week, to pour in fervid warnings from Tehcrán, the Governor-General was not likely to be allowed to sleep undisturbed by dreams of Russian aggression. A commercial mission he had already despatched to Kábul. Soon a political character would be added to it. He could only trust that Ranjít Singh would continue to be friendly; that the Amírs of Sind would show themselves amenable to his agent; above all, that Dost Muhammad Khán would fall into his plans, and thus enable him to complete the protection of his frontier, and to exchange guarantees of mutual assistance with the group of States between the Sutlej and Central Asia. If this could be achieved by the Indian Government, the instructions of the British Government would have been obeyed, and the safety of India secured.

With this hope in his heart, he watched anxiously the course of events. Shortly after the despatch of June 25 reached him, he had communicated to his masters in England his uneasiness at the direction which affairs were taking :—

'It is most annoying to me to learn,' he wrote on November 24, 1836, to the Chairman of the Court, 'that the Persians instead of strengthening themselves for defence,

and learning to practise good government at home, should
have engaged in wars of aggression to their eastward, and
should be throwing confusion into the countries of Herát,
Kandahár, and Kábul, where all was more than sufficiently
weak and unsettled before. I see no reason for direct interference in all this from this side; and we have nothing else
at present to do than to keep ourselves strong, and to wait
for occasion of using our influence.'

On the same date he writes to Sir John Hobhouse:

In the meantime, as this cloud becomes lighter' (the
threatened attack on Sind by the Mahárájá Ranjít Singh),
' one yet more threatening to the peace of these districts is
collecting in the further west, and the Persians are rapidly
advancing towards Herát. I am sorry for this. We are
feeding whatever there is of military strength in Persia,
that she may interfere with British objects; bring her own
and consequently Russian influence nearer to our frontier,
and throw into confusion and disorder all those countries in
which we were most anxious to see established tranquillity
and commerce. It is not easy for us to take any steps to
counteract this move from India, and I have heard nothing
from McNeill.'

For more than another year the Governor-General
watched his plans developing. From Captain Wade
at Ludhiána, from Colonel Pottinger at Haidarábád,
he continued to receive intelligence which led him
to believe that in the Punjab and Sind his policy
would be accepted. Captain Burnes was on his way
to Kábul, and on the success of his mission depended
the whole scheme. The corner-stone of the scheme
of frontier defence against ' the extension of Persian

dominion' and against 'Russian encroachments' was in Kábul. In February, 1837, Lord Auckland wrote to Mr. McNeill, deploring the imperfect nature of his information from that country. He still looked to commerce as the instrument by which possibly a better state of things might be brought about. Captain Burnes, he added, was on his way to Lahore and Kábul, to ask for facilities for annual fairs, and for the improvement of traffic on the Indus. If he could but gain time, he would not despair of seeing those countries flourishing and independent, and forming in their own strength the best rampart which India can have. On the 9th of April, Lord Auckland told Sir John Hobhouse that to Dost Muhammad he could only speak words of friend- liness, and, if he desired it, of mediation. 'In his pressing need, he has courted Persia, he has courted Russia, and he has courted us. But it would be madness in us, though we may wish to see his independence assured, to quarrel with the Sikhs for him.' Suddenly there flamed out beyond the Indus the 'blood-red blossom of war.' Dost Muhammad Khán had made a dash upon Peshawar, and on April 30, at the battle of Jamrúd, had been driven back. All hope of a friendly group of States on the north- west frontier was, at least for the moment, at an end. The breach between Kábul and Lahore was almost hopelessly widened. 'His ear of sagacity is closed by the cotton of negligence,' wrote Ranjít Singh of his rival. 'When it is of no avail to him, he will

bite the hand of sorrow with the teeth of repentance.'
Yet Lord Auckland still hoped.

On July 4th he wrote to the Chairman of the Court
of Directors that he looked for influence sufficient to
hold the rival powers on the British frontier in balance,
and prepared to unite in common defence. But
on September 8th he tells Sir John Hobhouse that
despatches from Lahore and Kábul inform him that
the Persian Embassy is daily expected in Kábul,
with a Russian in its train. Something less of the
spirit of accommodation, he adds, is seen in the last
letter of Dost Muhammad Khán to Burnes.

On the following day, September 9, 1837, the
Governor-General recorded a long Minute on Kábul
affairs. After describing the balance of parties in
Kábul, Kandahár, and Herát, so far as known to
him, he lays before his colleagues in Council the
final instructions which he would give to Captain
Burnes, who was about to enter Kábul. His mission,
he wrote, should be more political in character than
it had been hitherto considered to be, though with
no political power beyond that of transmitting any
proposition which appeared to him to be reasonable
through Captain Wade to his Government.

The Governor-General did not conceal his apprehension that the representations of Captain Burnes to
Dost Muhammad were likely to have but little effect at
the present moment. The Agent, upon a review of the
influence which he was likely to gain upon passing
events, should, he thought, decide upon the pro-

priety of prolonging his stay at Kábul; where, however, the information which he might be able to collect of the power, the means, and the state of parties in that country, could not but be useful.

On September 20, Captain Burnes entered Kábul, and the last link wanting in the chain to be stretched along the frontier would now, it was hoped, be forged. But the progress of events was not favourable to his success. On November 23, 1837, the day on which Lord Auckland and his camp left Benares, the Persian army commenced the siege of Herát. In December, Witkewitsch, a Russian emissary, appeared in Kábul, the bearer of a reply to Dost Muhammad's appeal of 1836 to St. Petersburg.

CHAPTER V

PRIVATE SECRETARY TO LORD AUCKLAND,
1838-1842

ON January 6 we find Lord Auckland writing to Sir John Hobhouse : 'Burnes is well established at Kábul, with only this disadvantage, that he can hardly hope that Dost Muhammad will be satisfied with anything that would not be offensive to Ranjít Singh ; and yet he ought to be satisfied that he is allowed to remain at peace, and is saved from actual invasion. But he is reckless, and intriguing, and will be difficult to keep quiet, as are the other Afgháns, and Sikhs, Herátees, Russians and Persians. It is a fine embroglio of diplomacy and intrigue, with more of bluster than of real strength anywhere. Yet it is impossible not to feel that the East and West are drawing sensibly nearer to each other.' The Governor-General of India probably began to wish that the burden of securing India against attack should be transferred to Cabinet shoulders. 'It is in Europe and in Persia,' wrote the Private Secretary to Captain Burnes on January 21, 'that the battle of Afghánistán must probably

be ultimately fought.' The words show how little
the Governor-General agreed with Lord Palmerston
that this 'was not an European but an Indian
question.' On February 8, Lord Auckland writes
to the Secret Committee that he is 'still inclined
to anticipate the adherence of Dost Muhammad to
British interests'; but the mission of a Russian agent
to Kábul demands, in his opinion, 'the serious consideration of the home authorities.' Trusting still to
form his rampart, he was not disposed, even if Herát
fell, at once to adopt an active policy, or to resort to
'any immediate interference by arms or money.' It
is evident that Lord Auckland in the spring of 1838
still hoped to obtain the alliance of Dost Muhammad,
and to form for India a zone of security through the
medium of allied powers on her frontiers. He would
thus have carried out his share in the joint policy,
and have given effect to the instructions of 1836. He
might then throw upon Great Britain the settlement
of her struggle with Russia for ascendency in Persian
counsels at Teherán.

Sir John Kaye has insisted much on the position that,
while Russia and Persia were making large promises
and holding out great hopes to Dost Muhammad
Khán, Captain Burnes had nothing to tender but
assurances of goodwill. This, if containing an element
of truth, is far from being the whole truth. What
Russia may have promised is conjectural. Dost Muhammad was assured by Captain Burnes of protection
against Sikh and Persian. But the Amír did not fear

the Sikh, and the Persian was a long way off.
Captain Burnes had that which, though not his to
give, the Amír thought that it was in his power to
obtain. Although Peshawar belonged not to the East
India Company but to Ranjít Singh, and had never
belonged to Dost Muhammad, the Company could, if it
chose, cajole or force the Sikhs into parting with it.
Unless Peshawar were placed by Lord Auckland in
the hollow of Dost Muhammad's hand, it very soon
became evident that Captain Burnes might retrace his
steps to India. The Amír would, if desired, pay a
tribute for Peshawar to the Mahárájá. He would
hold it, if need be, conjointly with his brother, its
late ruler, Sultán Muhammad Khán. But if Lord
Auckland desired his alliance, in one or another
fashion Peshawar must be 'conveyed' to him. It
was on that account that he had addressed himself to Lord Auckland, to Persia, and the Czar.
Peshawar must be his. That was his ultimatum.
There was no getting behind it. On that rock
the negotiation split. Dost Muhammad Khán
would not even leave the matter of Peshawar to
the friendly discretion of the Governor-General.
He would make it a *sine quâ non* of his good
understanding, whether with Ranjít Singh or Lord
Auckland.

Ranjít Singh is believed to have been willing to
make over Peshawar, on terms, to Sultán Muhammad
Khán, the Amír's brother, who alone had been its ruler
before the Sikhs obtained possession of it. But this

Dost Muhammad would not listen to. He would rather even that it remained in Sikh hands. Of Ranjít Singh's power to invade him in Kábul he had little fear, he said to Captain Burnes ; ' Of his power to injure me if he reinstate Sultán Muhammad Khán in the government of Peshdwar, I have great apprehension ; for in it I see a Muhammadan ruler instead of a Sikh.' It may be that Lord Auckland was not averse from having a considerable Sikh garrison locked up in Peshdwar. But he remembered also that he had very recently frustrated the designs of Ranjít Singh on Sind. He could not again give him check without risk of serious rupture. The value of the Sikh alliance, seeing that its powerful army lay upon our frontier, was unquestionable. He had little faith in the loyalty of Dost Muhammad ; believing that, if installed at Peshdwar, he would allow himself to be bound by obligation neither to Sikh nor to British. For his part, Dost Muhammad Khán hungered for Peshdwar with a desire which nothing but possession could appease. When war broke out a few years later between the Sikhs and the British, Dost Muhammad and his horsemen descended into the Peshdwar valley. When in 1857 the Government of India was locked in deadly struggle with its rebel army, Sir John Lawrence, searching with all his great knowledge of men and matters in the Punjab for means of securing his North-West frontier from attack in the last resort, and of withdrawing its British garrison to the trenches before Delhi, knew of no surer way than that of making over to Dost Muhammad the coveted valley of Peshawar.

'I have been sorry to see,' wrote the Private Secretary to Captain Burnes on February 7, 1838, 'that you still cling to the idea of the abandonment of Peshawar, even in its civil government, by Ranjit Singh. He has given us no indication that he has the slightest intention of the kind. He may be possibly brought to make over the administration of the territory to the Sultán Muhammad Khán; but Dost Muhammad Khán can exercise no interference on the point. This should be understood distinctly and definitely.'

Again on March 14 the Private Secretary recurs to the subject under the Governor-General's instructions :—

'You will see that it is a principal object with the Governor-General to ascertain, what does not clearly appear from the papers yet before him, whether Dost Muhammad Khán intends to make under all circumstances a *sine quâ non* of possessing some share in the Peshawar territory. Apprized as you now are of his Lordship's fixed opinions, you will, he is quite satisfied, use every endeavour to dissuade Dost Muhammad from persisting in such a resolution. . . .

'The question is, whether Dost Muhammad would prefer renouncing his connexion with us, that he may retain a barren claim to a portion of the Peshawar territory, to leaving the Sikh in the immediate occupation of that country, under the continued exercise of our influence for his safety in his Kábul dominions. . . .

'If Dost Muhammad should wish his scheme of having a share in Peshawar to be freely discussed, though without making a *sine quâ non* of it, this, I dare say, will readily be done. While it is thought (you will see) that advantage will arise from his opening the negotiation directly, if we can bring about a readiness to come to terms on both sides, they may more easily arrange the details for themselves than we can for them.'

After Captain Burnes had left Kábul in April, 1838, and was on his way to India, on May 22 the Governor-General finally caused him to be addressed in these terms:—

'You dwell on the long silence as to the feelings of Ranjít Singh regarding Peshávar. But you will remember that it was distinctly stated in instructions of the 20th of January and 7th of March that Dost Muhammad must first disclaim all intention of making a *sine quâ non* of the restoration (or more properly the cession) to him, wholly or partially, of Peshávar, before we could enter at all seriously on the subject with Ranjít Singh. That disclaimer, it is needless to say, he has never made; and in the end he has insisted on pretensions in a spirit directly the reverse, so that for the result he has only to accuse himself.'

From the position which Dost Muhammad had taken up Captain Burnes was totally unable to drive him. He saw that the Amír was a man of paramount influence in Afghánistán, whose alliance could be of the greatest value to us. But in order that we should make him our friend it was necessary that we should make Ranjít Singh our enemy. That, in Lord Auckland's judgment, would be madness. The promises lavished by the Russian agent at Kábul, combined with daily expectation of the fall of Herát, and of the discomfiture of British policy, had rendered Dost Muhammad impracticable.

Ranjít Singh's friendship Lord Auckland judged to
be far more valuable than the goodwill of the Amír.
The Sikh army was very powerful, and lay close to
our borders.   The friendship of Kábul, if Lahore
was hostile, would be comparatively of little use,
even if it could be counted on.   Hence the Governor-
General would put no pressure on Ranjít Singh nor
filch from him the price of Dost Muhammad's alliance.
On April 26, 1838, the English agent left Kábul;
the Russian remained.

While Captain Burnes was retracing his steps, there
passed over India one of those periodical waves of
emotion with which all who are acquainted with
the Peninsula are familiar.   It stretched from the
Sutlej to Mysore, from Bombay to the Nepál boundary.
These movements resemble the tremor which passes
from time to time throughout the range of the Himálayas, rarely resulting in upheaval or disturbance,
but indicating the presence of forces never dormant.
With a Persian army accompanied by a Russian
minister at Herát, and a Russian emissary at Kábul,
such a phenomenon was too significant to be disregarded.   In the remotest Deccan natives began to
bury jewels, money, and valuables in the ground.
General Cubbon reported great uneasiness in Mysore,
Major Sutherland in Gwalior, Colonel Skinner in
Hansi.   Emissaries from Nepál were making their
way to Lahore and Kábul, breathing mischief.   The
public securities fell.   Muhammadan news-sheets published appeals to the faithful against the rule of the

unbeliever. Men's minds were failing them for fear.
In the village, the bazár, the great man's reception-
rooms, there was a pleasurable expectation that some
novel excitement was about to be felt. It gave evidence of the eagerness with which events beyond the
frontier were followed by natives. To Lord Auckland it was an argument in favour of a vigorous
policy.

McNeill had hurried off on March 8 to Herát, in the
hope of staying hostilities. Before leaving Teherán he
was careful to point out, in a letter received about the
time when Captain Burnes left Kábul, that the Sháh
had been able for four months to feed 48,000 men in
his camp before Herát, notwithstanding the efforts
made by the Herát Government to carry off or destroy
the supplies which the country afforded. This was
proof that a hostile army might move throughout the
valley without suffering from want. It gave in his
eyes additional importance to the position of Herát,
and to the influence which the Power that holds it
may exercise over the security of India. From London
came also the voice of apprehension and warning;
'We have made an effort, in which we cannot fail,'
wrote Sir John Hobhouse in a letter received on
May 4, 'without compromising the dignity of the
British Crown and diminishing the national influence,
not only in Persia but in all the countries towards
the western frontier of India.'

Throughout the preceding months Lord Auckland
had been in close and constant communication with

Captain Burnes and with Captain Wade. It is not
in the scheme of these pages to comment on the merits
of any of the prominent actors of that time, or to
weigh one with another. Each, as far as possible,
speaks in his own words. No two men differed more
in their views of policy than Captain Wade and
Captain Burnes. One was all for Sháh Shujá, the
other for Dost Muhammad. Captain Wade, 'from the
best sources of information open to him, believed that
the Amír was by no means popular. The greater
part of his troops were disaffected and insubordinate.'
Captain Burnes, on the other hand, conceived that
the Amír was 'a man of undoubted ability, who had
at heart a high opinion of the British nation.' But
however much they might disagree on the merits of
Dost Muhammad, on one point they expressed themselves in identical language. If Sháh Shujá-ul-Mulk
were sent back to Kábul with a mere personal
guard of British troops he would be received with
open arms. 'There is little doubt,' wrote Wade,
quoting Masson, 'but that if (on the occasion of Sháh
Shujá's last attempt on Kábul) a single British officer
had accompanied him, not as an ally and coadjutor,
but as a mere reporter of proceedings to his own
Government, his simple appearance would have been
sufficient to have procured the Sháh's re-establish-
ment.' Masson was an Englishman who, for private
reasons, had passed twelve years in Kábul, and was
believed to be familiar with the temper of the people.
In his view Captain Wade expressed entire con-

currence. Captain Burnes, though he hotly contended
for the Amír, held the same opinion as to the greeting
which Sháh Shujá would meet with.

As for Sháh Shujá,' he wrote in the letter just referred to,
'the British Government has only to send him to Peshawar
with an agent and two of its own regiments as an honorary
escort, and an avowal to the Afgháns that we have taken up
his cause, to ensure his being fixed for ever on his throne.
The present time (he wrote on June 2, 1838) is perhaps
better than any previous to it, for the Afgháns, as a nation,
detest Persia; and Dost Muhammad Khán's having gone
over to the Court of Teherán, though he believes it to be
from dire necessity, converts many a doubting Afghán into
a bitter enemy. The Mahárájá's permission has only to be
asked for the ex-king's advance to Peshawar, granting him
at the same time some four or five of his regiments which
have no Sikhs in their ranks, and Shujá becomes king.
He need not move from Peshawar, but address the Khai-
baris, the Kohistánis of Kábul, and all the Afgháns, from
that city, that he has the co-operation of the British and the
Mahárájá; and with but a little distribution of ready money,
say two or three lakhs of rupees, he will find himself the
real king of the Afgháns in a couple of months.'

A few days later, in the course of replies to a series
of questions put to him by Mr. Macnaghten, Captain
Burnes stated his conviction that Sháh Shujá would
be joined by a considerable portion of Dost Muhammad's troops, as well as by the people of the country.
The testimony of Captain Burnes was peculiarly
significant, because he was a witness hostile to Sháh
Shujá. His vows were all for Dost Muhammad. When

Captain Burnes used language such as has been quoted, Lord Auckland must have felt that very little doubt could be entertained as to the reception which Sháh Shujá, if reinstated in Kábul, would meet with.

With the withdrawal of Captain Burnes from Kábul in April, 1838, the combination which Lord Auckland, in 1837, had hoped for, fell finally to the ground. He had not only failed to draw Dost Muhammad into an alliance with Great Britain, but had left him in the arms of Russia and Persia. Witkewitsch had arrived in Kábul after Captain Burnes, but remained an honoured guest when the British Agent had been compelled to leave it. The Russian Minister was pressing the siege of Herát; Russian volunteers were engaged in it. On May 6 it seemed 'scarcely within hope Herát could escape.' Major Leech, the English Agent, had been made to leave Kandahár. All India was expectant; the English Cabinet watchful. MᶜNeill was beside himself with apprehension. The despatch of June 25 was burning the Governor-General's pocket. What had been the result of his 'immediate and most earnest attention' as to the measures to be taken 'to prevent the extension of Persian dominion in that quarter, or to raise a timely barrier against the encroachments of Russian influence'? Since that date nearly two years had passed, and the present state of affairs was infinitely more critical than any which prevailed when these instructions had been received by him. Not only had the desired barrier not been raised, but a highway had been opened by Kábul to Persia and to Russia. The situation, so far as Lord Auckland could at that time see it, was this. On the one side the Cabinet of Great Britain had failed to establish its influence with the Court of Persia. On the other, the Indian Government had been baffled in Kábul. The efforts made, on either hand, during the two years which had elapsed since the despatch of June 25, 1836, was penned, had signally failed. Neither at Herát nor in Kábul had British policy succeeded in its aims. Mr. McNeill was discredited in Persia, and Captain Burnes had been withdrawn from Afghánistán. It could not be known at Simla what course would be pursued by the Cabinet in its discomfiture ; but the time had arrived when it seemed unavoidable that, for his part, Lord Auckland should 'interfere decidedly in the affairs of Afghánistán.'

On May 12, 1838, the Governor-General put the position before himself in a Minute, and recorded the measures which he thought it best to take. The Minute has been published in Blue-books, and space does not admit of its being inserted here. Reviewing at great length the events which had led to the situation as it then stood, Lord Auckland proceeded to consider the several courses open to him. His policy had been to replace the Persian alliance of 1814 by a belt of defence consisting of allied native States on the frontier—by a 'rampart,' as he called it—and to leave the British Cabinet to regain by

diplomacy its influence in Teherán. That having
failed, interference from India might become necessary. But it need not necessarily be the interference
of the Government of India. If Dost Muhammad
would not join the alliance, he must make room
for another. Lord Auckland now looked to making
use of the agency of Ranjít Singh and Sháh Shujá.
It was not unless the former declined to be made
use of, or the latter was found to be unequal to the
task of recovering for himself his kingdom, that
direct British agency could be thought of. Even
should this become necessary, he wrote later to Sir
John Hobhouse, 'a friendly power and an intimate
connexion in Afghánistán, a peaceful alliance with
Lahore, and an established influence in Sind, are
objects for which some hazards may well be run.'

'I would not commit myself now,' Lord Auckland wrote,
'to any course of action. But we must prepare to meet the
serious difficulty which is hanging over us with a promptitude adequate to the occasion; and it is well, therefore, to
follow out the several plans which are open to us in some
fullness of detail. If Persia should succeed against Herát,
and advance upon Eastern Afghánistán, we have, as it
appears to me, but three courses to follow: the first, to
confine our defensive measures to the line of the Indus, and
to leave Afghánistán to its fate; the second, to attempt to
save Afghánistán by granting succour to the existing Chief-
ships of Kábul and Kandahár; the third, to permit or to
encourage the advance of Ranjít Singh's armies upon Kábul
under counsel and restriction, and (as subsidiary to his
advance) to organize an expedition headed by Sháh Shujá-

ul-Mulk, such as I have above explained. The first course
would be absolute defeat and would leave a free opening to
Russian and Persian intrigue upon our frontier. The second
would be only to give power to those who feel greater animosity against the Sikhs than they do against the Persians,
and who would probably use against the former the means
placed at their disposal. And the third course which, even
in the event of the successful resistance of Herât, would
appear to be most expedient, would, if that State were to
fall into the hands of the Persians, have yet more to
recommend it, and I cannot hesitate to say that the inclina-
tion of my opinion is, for the reasons which will be gathered
from these papers, very strongly in favour of it.'

The measure adopted, in pursuance of this Minute,
was the mission to Lahore of Mr. Macnaghten, Chief
Secretary to Lord Auckland's Government. The
Mahárájá was at Adínanagar, beyond Lahore, and
there in May, 1838, Mr. Macnaghten repaired, to be
met by Captain Burnes, now on his return from
Kábul, by Captain Wade, and by others. The instructions given to Mr. Macnaghten were, briefly, these.
Alternative courses of action were to be laid before
the Mahárájá. Either the joint treaty executed between Ranjít Singh and Sháh Shujá in 1833, when,
in conjunction with the former, Sháh Shujá had
made his last descent on Kábul, should be recognized by the British Government. In that case a
Sikh force, accompanied by British agents, would
' advance cautiously on Kábul.' At the same time,
a division of the British army, escorting Sháh
Shujá, would temporarily occupy Shikárpur in Sind.

Money would be advanced to Sháh Shujá wherewith to levy troops and purchase arms; and the services of British officers would be lent him. This failing to meet the Mahárájá's views, he would be allowed ' to take his own course against Dost Muhammad Khán, without reference to us.' In that case Sháh Shujá would return to Kábul only in the event of the Mahárájá wishing to make an instrument of him, and in such case, again, only ' with the almost assured certainty of success.' ' His Lordship,' it was added, ' on the whole is disposed to think that the plan which is second in order is that which will be found most expedient.' The Mahárájá was, in fact, to pull the chestnuts out of the fire. In Persian metaphor, which evidently much tickled Lord Auckland, the beak of appetite was to be tempted by the fruit of conquest and the berries of revenge.

Scarcely had Mr. Macnaghten arrived in the plains before he wrote the first of a series of letters, pressing upon the Governor-General reconsideration of these instructions. These letters, yellow in hue, soiled by damp and dust, and in parts barely legible with their faded ink, show that Lord Auckland was little disposed to yield his judgment to that of his secretary. On May 21, 22, 24, 26, 27, 28, 29, and 31, and on June 1, 2, and 4, Mr. Macnaghten exhausts himself in repeating and in reinforcing his arguments. The more he reflected on the present state of affairs the more he felt satisfied that it would be highly impolitic to let Ranjít Singh take up Sháh Shujá without British partnership. His views, says the Chief Secretary, have the concurrence of Wade and Mackeson, the two officers to whose judgment is due the greatest deference from their peculiar knowledge of the Mahárájá's character. There is no safe middle course. Either the Government of India must act strictly on the defensive, trusting to its own power to repel invasion, and to a fortuitous concurrence of events to frustrate the intrigues of Russia and Persia on its western frontier; or it must take arms against this sea of troubles, and, by opposing, end them. It was not practicable that Sháh Shujá could be restored to the throne of Kábul by Sikh bayonets. Were he so restored, the last state of Kábul would be worse than the first. Day by day the Chief Secretary repeats these arguments, pressing for leave to tell Ranjít Singh that, 'with or without the co-operation of the Mahárájá, the Government of India will set up Sháh Shujá.' Lord Auckland was not to be hurried. If Wade and Mackeson were right in their estimate of Ranjít Singh, he replied, co-operation with him was not to be hoped for. On the other hand, though it might be well, by opposing troubles, to end them, it might be as well too, to consider whether we are not flying to others that we know not of. ' Our ignorance of what is passing in the Persian camp, the obscure responsibility of the Government here in regard to Persia and to European politics, and the measure which I take of hazards to be incurred, would lead me much rather to stand still, as nearly as circumstances

will allow me to do so, than at once to take the plunge
to which you would urge me. ... I much prefer this
course to one which might combine all Sikh feeling
against us ; and which might at once pledge honour,
and strength, and finance to the, I think, uncertain
cause of Sháh Shujá, in a war to be carried on 600
miles from our frontier. To this consummation we
may have to come at last; but I would at least see
my way more clearly than I do at present before I
venture onwards.'

'To arrest the Persian advance by the advance of our own
troops and by the support of Sháh Shujá,' he adds in a later
letter, 'are measures, not which we are disposed to carry
into effect at all hazards, but which we may be compelled
to ; and all the means of executing which we most reasonably
and strongly desire to keep at our own disposal.'

On June 7, Lord Auckland learned that Ranjít
Singh had declared promptly for co-operation; and
had declined to be drawn, alone and single-handed,
into a march to Kábul. The alternative of action
through Sháh Shujá remained. Confronted with
this alternative the Governor-General could not but
pause. He hoped to get information from England,
which might relieve him of direct responsibility.
Possibly he might learn that diplomacy at Tehérán
had rendered the employment of force on the Indus
unnecessary. He is 'pleased that Mr. Macnaghten
had not absolutely pledged him to the alternative
course, for, as you will know, I would gladly pause

before I take a step in a measure of so much importance which I might not be able to retrace, and upon which instructions are now to be expected within a fortnight from England. A better sight into the state of political feeling in Afghánistán, or events passing on the side of Persia, may make further consideration most desirable.'

Three days later, on June 10, Lord Auckland wrote to Mr. Macnaghten :—

'You must not, however, be surprised that I yet see hazards and difficulties upon which my mind must hesitate, and of which we may take different measure. . . . When once the determination is made I shall be with you for promptitude of action, and perhaps even for greater promptitude of action than you may be.'

About the same time he writes to Sir John Hobhouse that as to the affairs of the Punjab, Afghánistán, and Persia, owing to want of information as to the progress of affairs in Europe, he has never felt any confidence in himself, and has known himself to be liable to error at every step. He has been playing in the dark, and with his hands tied, a game requiring a clear-sighted vigour. For some time he has not heard from McNeill, and can only conjecture by what counter engagements made with Persia, engagements on his side of Afghánistán may be embarrassed, or by what new dangers too passive delay may be attended.

'The obscure responsibility of the Government here in regard to Persia and European politics' is the keynote of the Governor-General's hesitation. He cannot conjecture what is passing in London, in Teherán, or at Herát. It takes six or seven months to get replies from any of these places. Now that he is within visible distance of war, he cannot but again ask himself whose interests are to be mainly served by it. Those of India, perhaps; but has England, as mistress of India, no interests in her dependency? Is it wholly an ' Indian question '? Will England not exert herself too? The road to India through Persia having been thrown open, by Teherán, to a European Power, will not England, acting from Europe, endeavour to replace the barriers of 1814? Herát, so far as he knows, has not fallen, and that last compulsion has not been put upon him. He could wish, with all his heart, ' that the authorities in England had a better sense of some of the difficulties against which he had to contend.' Though he knows the lines of the Ministry's policy, he can get from them no indication of the precise course which they would now wish him to follow. Little wonder that he hesitates; hopes for instructions from England, or intelligence from Teherán; and would gladly pause for a fortnight, and await instructions, before he takes a measure of such importance as making India the Foreign Secretary's stalking-horse.

To add to his doubts, his Secretary in Calcutta, Mr. H. T. Prinsep, is warning him of Sháh Shujá's personal incapacity. Mr. Macnaghten is to consult with Captain Wade whether there is remedy for this in the character and popularity of any of his family. Captain Burnes, Mr. Masson, Dr. Lord, and Mr. Wood, all men conversant with Kábul affairs, are to be asked for their opinion on the feeling regarding Sháh Shujá among the Afgháns, and as to his probable means of maintaining himself.

Pending Mr. Macnaghten's return nothing had been decided. On July 10 Lord Auckland wrote to Mr. McNeill, expressing the extreme anxiety he had felt to receive accounts of a later date than March 7, that he might know what was passing at home, and shape his plans accordingly. 'But I must do my best, without having this advantage, and I have nearly formed my decision.' It seemed most probable at that date that, in conjunction with Ranjít Singh, he might 'have to surround Sháh Shujá with British officers, and support him in an attempt to re-establish himself in Afghánistán. I need not recapitulate to you the many considerations which seem to me to justify this course; nor, on the other hand, those which may make me adopt it only with extreme reluctance.' The next day (July 11) he tells Mac-naghten that till he comes back no plans will be formed. On the 12th he sends Macnaghten 'a rough sketch of what appears to me the maximum of military operations which may become necessary.' The sketch has not been preserved; but a letter from Mr. Colvin of the same date says that 5,000 British troops are talked of. 'Rabbles of raw levies got together at much cost by Sháh Shujá, and not to be depended on,' are looked on as questionable. There must be 'no chance of failure.' At the best, months would pass before Sháh Shujá, if left solely to his own resources, would be ready to move, and meanwhile Herát might fall, and Kandahár be occupied. On July 10 has been received a despatch of March 20 from the Secret Committee, saying that Lord Palmerston has authorized Mr. McNeill to leave Persia if redress is not afforded for an insult to his courier. In that event the Committee 'leave it discretional with you to adopt such measures as may seem to you expedient to meet the contingency of the cessation of our relations with the Court of Persia.' On July 12 Lord Auckland tells Sir John Hobhouse :—

'All that I am doing, or preparing to do, is well justified by the avowed policy of the Persian Court and by the hostile proceeding of the Russian agents; and you may assume it for next to certain that I shall go onwards, with many a deep feeling of regret that I am not allowed to prosecute measures of peace and of peaceful improvement, but with a perfect conviction that it is only by a bold front, and by strong exertion, that the aggressions and the dangers with which we are threatened can be warded off. I can decide absolutely on nothing until Macnaghten's return, and I think that I shall then be able to see my way clearly to all that is to be done, and with no fear of the result, though I shall be sorry for the money which it will cost.'

On the 14th, Mr. Colvin, writing to Mr. Prinsep, says, 'We expect him (Macnaghten) at Simla with Burnes in three or four days.' On the 19th he has returned.

With the return of Mr. Macnaghten to Simla, the question of the form which the expedition to Kábul should take could not be long delayed. The 'Tripartite Treaty,' as it came to be called, was signed on June 26 by Ranjít Singh, on July 16 by Sháh Shujá, at Ludhiána, and on July 19 was placed by Mr. Macnaghten before Lord Auckland. The treaty was the secret of Polichinelle. The Sikhs knew its terms; Sháh Shujá had at once set to work to call together his friends ; all India had followed Mr. Macnaghten's movements; before many days Dost Muhammad would be preparing for war. The winter was approaching, when, for many months, military operations would become impossible in Kábul. By July 28 the decision to send a force across the Indus was communicated to the Governor of Bombay. 'Not less than 5,000 men' (to be increased as the information received may show to be necessary) 'are arranged for.' 'Such a measure,' it is added, 'would never of course be thought of, if the cause of Sháh Shujá were not generally popular among the Afgháns.' But upon this point all opinion coincides. As Dr. Lord writes, 'There never was anything which might more properly be termed a national sentiment than the feeling for Sháh Shujá's restoration.' The number is increased in August to 14,000 men, besides a smaller contingent from Bombay. The Commander-in-Chief would not assent to the despatch of a force of which the numbers did not guarantee him from all reasonable risk of disaster.

On August 13 was sent to the Court the long Despatch, since published, which contains Lord Auckland's vindication of his policy. He had been deeply sensible, he wrote in his despatch, of the responsibility which his decision placed upon him:

'But I have felt, after the most anxious deliberation, that I could not otherwise rightly acquit myself of my trust; and a reference to the despatches of your Honourable Committee of June 25, 1836, and May 10 last, have led me to look with confidence for your general approbation and support to the plans on which, in the exercise of the discretion confided to me, I have resolved.'

Reference in these terms and at such a crisis of affairs, to the despatch of June 25, is sufficient proof of the sense in which Lord Auckland interpreted the discretion left to him by the Board of Control, and of the alternative which he conceived it to indicate.

The despatch of May 10, 1838, to which Lord Auckland made reference conjointly with that of June 25, 1836, was received by him on July 16. A few days later, he decided to send a British force into Kábul. Although he regarded this later despatch as furnishing evidence that his action was in accordance with the policy of the Cabinet, its language is less uncompromising than that of June. Its terms are as follows :—

'We have received a letter from the Governor-General, addressed to us in the Secret Department, dated February 8, last, with its 127 enclosures.

'We entirely concur with you in thinking that the arrival of a Russian envoy at Kábul, bearing a letter from the

Emperor Nicholas to Dost Muhammad, is an event demanding your special attention, but we also agree with you in concluding that Capt. Burnes exceeded the instructions given to him, and manifested an anxiety which might defeat his own objects in entering into premature engagements with the Afghán Princes.

'We approve of your instructing Capt. Burnes to withdraw from Kábul, if contrary to his advice and remonstrance Dost Muhammad should formally accept from the Russian envoy of those offers of assistance which are stated to be contained in the letter of the Emperor Nicholas to Dost Muhammad.

'At the same time we must observe that the letter of the Russian Emperor was an answer to an application made to that sovereign by the Ruler of Kábul, and that in dealing with this matter it will be advisable to avoid any proceedings which may give rise to a controversy with the Russian Ambassador at Teherán, or with the Court of St. Petersburg.

'The last despatches from Constantinople have informed us that Mr. McNeill was about to proceed on March 10 to the Persian headquarters before Herát, from which it may be inferred that he has received satisfaction for the outrage committed on the messenger attached to the British Mission.

'We are anxiously waiting for a detailed account of the circumstances which have induced Mr. McNeill to resolve upon his announced journey, and of all matters connected with the operations of the Sháh against Herát. Until we shall have received these communications, and been informed of the actual state of things in that quarter, it would be premature to come to any decision upon the affairs of Afghánistán. We are aware of the difficulties arising out of the late Treaty, by which we have stipulated not to interfere between Persia and the Afgháns unless at the express desire of both parties; but we do not conceal from you that it may become a question for the British Government to consider whether, if Persia should persevere in her plans of conquest in Afghánistán, and should appear likely to succeed in them, the danger thence resulting to Great Britain would be greater than the security which might be derived from that other stipulation of the before-named Treaty, by which the Sháh undertakes to prevent any European army from traversing Persia in order to invade British India.

'In that case we might feel ourselves called upon to declare the whole Treaty at an end; but as such a step would be a departure from the usual practice, it would be more agreeable to us to learn that the Sháh had consented voluntarily to an amended Treaty, in preparing which, Mr. McNeill has, as you are aware, received instructions to omit the embarrassing article relative to Afghánistán.'

The long succession of events which led up to this decision has been thus traced, though with needful brevity, step by step. It has been seen how the chain of incidents stretches back to England and 1814; is taken up, in 1828, by Russia; links itself later, by Teherán and Herát, to Kábul; and so, in 1836, passes finally through the Punjab into Lord Auckland's hands. The converging influences have been indicated; the apprehensions, namely, of the British Cabinet, speaking through the Board of Control; the ambition of Persia; the intrigues of Russia, the greed of Dost Muhammad. We have seen how, in pursuance of Sir John Hobhouse's instructions, the Burnes mission passed from a commercial into a political colour. We have watched Lord Auckland throughout 1837 in communication with the Board of Control, keeping that body informed of his endeavours to give effect to the instructions received by him. The gradual failure of his efforts, which were foredoomed by the untimely battle of Jamrúd, but which continued in spite of that complication, has been traced ; their final issue in the withdrawal of Burnes has been described. The erection of a ' rampart ' on the North-West frontier of India has been shown to have been Lord Auckland's policy. When the Amír refused to have a hand in it, the measures consequent on his attitude have been narrated. It has been seen that Ranjít Singh would not accept the burden of invading Kábul; and that no confidence was felt in Sháh Shujá's capacity to levy within sufficient time the troops necessary to that end, or to lead them to success when raised. But the treaty had been signed. At Herát, in India, in Afghánistán, were grounds for urgency. From the political as well as the military point of view, a decision must be taken. No further light could be looked for from London or Teherán. No aid apparently could be hoped for from England. The responsibility had been laid by the home authorities on India alone of combating the 'extension of Persian dominion and the encroachments of Russian influence.' The day had arrived when, though Lord Auckland would gladly have paused, that responsibility compelled a decision.

This is not a history of the first Afghán war. That event is dealt with in these pages, only so far as is necessary for the purpose of this Memoir. If, in exposing the trivial point of view which would

attribute the Afghán war to the pernicious influence
of the three Secretaries who had accompanied Lord
Auckland to Upper India, the policy which led to it
is found to have originated not at Simla, but in
London, the consequences which followed must be
laid on shoulders other than those of Lord Auckland.
But all that is needful here to remind the reader is
that the aim of this narrative is to trace out, as
against the fly-moving-the-wheel theory of Sir John
Kaye, the several elements of which the action taken
by Lord Auckland was the outcome.   It is not sought
to apportion responsibility between the several statesmen concerned; still less to express an opinion as to
the merits of the policy pursued.

In the course of October there issued the much discussed Proclamation, bearing date October 1, which
decreed the fall of Dost Muhammad Khán. 'It would
have been much more effective,' wrote Lord Auckland,
'if I had not had the fear of Downing Street before
my eyes.'   The real motives which led to the war are
as studiously kept out of sight in that Proclamation
as they were afterwards rigorously snipped out of
the sheets which appeared in the first Afghán Blue
Book.   Diplomatic susceptibilities must be consulted.
There must be no mention of Russia, though the action
of Russia on Persia was the *causa causans.*   There
must be no allusion to instructions from England;
above all, not a whisper of the despatch of 1836.
It is purely a quarrel between the Government of
India and Dost Muhammad. 'The King hath run bad

humours on the Knight; and that's the even of it.' Such a state paper was of course much criticized. It bears traces evident enough of reserve. High authorities, however, the Military Member of Council (Colonel Morison), and Mr. Farish, the acting Governor of Bombay, are shown by Mr. Colvin's Diary to have approved it. The same pages, quoting Mr. Robertson, a member of the Governor-General's Council, prove that he had been already converted by the despatch of August 13. 'The chairman of the Court of Directors,' wrote Sir John Hobhouse later to Lord Auckland, 'thought it an admirable document.' In his History of India, published twenty years later, Mr. Marshman writes:—

'Beyond the Ministerial circle in Downing Street, and the Secretaries at Simla, this preposterous enterprise was universally condemned as soon as it was announced.'

But when the Proclamation issued he wrote to Mr. Colvin saying that Lord Auckland's measures must commend themselves to every one who knew anything of the present position. The more circumstances were developed, he added, the more does the necessity of his course appear.

The entries in Mr. Colvin's Diary are apparently at variance with Sir John Kaye's statement, that when the Proclamation was sent to Calcutta, there issued from the Council Chamber a respectful remonstrance against the consummation of a measure of such importance, without an opportunity being afforded to the

Counsellors of recording their opinions upon it. The remonstrance, he adds, went to England, and elicited an assurance to the effect that Lord Auckland could have intended no personal slight to the members of the Supreme Council.

The writer has been unable to trace this remonstrance. Sir John Kaye has given no authority for his statement, and has offered no clue to the documents containing either the alleged remonstrance, or the reply. There is nothing to show whether the collective Council, or one or more members, remonstrated. Sir John Kaye's assertion must be taken for what it may be worth. The only document available, besides Mr. Colvin's Diary, seems to be irreconcilable with that assertion. The Proclamation of October 1 was forwarded to England under cover of a letter of that date. The reply of the Board of Control is dated December 26. It makes no allusion to any such protest as is referred to in the passage quoted ; but, on the contrary, in its final paragraph, it says—

'We are much pleased to find that the Governor-General of India and the Supreme Council cordially agree in all the measures in contemplation, not only for the protection of the North-West frontier, but also with reference to the possible necessity of undertaking warlike operations against Ava and Nepál.'

There is no hint here of discord. Not agreement only, but cordial agreement is indicated. Whatever the purport of the remonstrance may have been, or from whomsoever it emanated. it seems clear that

Lord Auckland had communicated his projects to his Council, and had secured its approval.

'Had you received our Despatch of October 24 before your Proclamation issued,' wrote Sir John Hobhouse a little later to Lord Auckland, 'you would have had nothing to say except that you had taken the course in pursuance of orders from home.' When the news of Captain Burnes' departure from Kábul reached London, the hesitation which Lord Auckland had felt does not seem to have embarrassed the Cabinet. They resolved at once to wage war. As the war which they resolved upon was to be waged vicariously, their alacrity raises less surprise. They had waited since June, 1836. They had seen, matters going from worse to worse. At last they learned that the British Agent had left Kábul, and that the Russian emissary remained, an honoured guest. Then, on October 24, they sent out orders which fully explained what had been at the back of their thoughts when two years previously they had addressed Lord Auckland. The President of the Board of Control requested Lord Auckland 'to consider that Despatch as containing the deliberate opinion of the Queen's Government, assented to after much discussion and previous correspondence between the different departments, and most cordially concurred in by the present authorities at the India Office.' The first half of the Despatch deals with a project of invading Persia which Mr. McNeill had advocated, but which the Foreign Secretary promptly set aside. Such a project was in truth, the

last which could have commended itself to him. It
would have involved Great Britain directly in the
quarrel. It would have thrown Persia into the
arms of Russia; it would have led Great Britain into
diplomatic, possibly into military collision with the
Western Power. What the Foreign Office wished
was indeed the reverse of what Mr. Colvin in his
letter of January 21, 1838, to Burnes had anticipated.
It was in Afghánistán that the battle of Europe and
of Persia was to be fought. Owing to its length, so
much only of the Despatch can be here printed as
deals with an expedition to Kábul; and of that again
so much only as is most material. The instructions
which were conveyed to Lord Auckland differ so far,
it will be seen, from the course which he pursued, in
that they leave him discretion to make another effort
to gain over Dost Muhammad and his brothers. Possibly such an effort might have succeeded. On the
other hand, Lord Auckland's distrust of the Bárakzáis, the unshaken influence of Russia at Teherán, and
the effect in India of the withdrawal of the British
Agent from Kábul in the circumstances which accompanied it, might have seemed to Lord Auckland to
be a bar to the resumption of negotiations. Be this
as it may, when the Despatch arrived on January 16,
1839, war had been declared; the army was on its
way; the Government of India was pledged to its
policy. All bridges of retreat had been broken.

' 14. We have heard,' wrote the Secret Committee, ' with
the utmost regret that the Mission to Kábul, conducted by

Lieut.-Col. Sir Alexander Burnes, has failed, and that Major Leech, who was accredited to the Court of Kandahár, has also been obliged to return from that city. Still more concerned have we been to find that a Russian agent has been openly received at Kábul, and that the Sirdárs of Kandahár have entered into a Treaty with the Sháh of Persia, by which the Sháh consents to establish the power of the Sirdárs in Herát under certain conditions, and that the Ambassador of the Emperor of Russia has, under his own hand, bound himself to secure the fulfilment of the Treaty.

'15. It is obvious that such an engagement is altogether at variance with British interests in Central Asia, and that should Herát fall into the hands of the Sháh and be delivered over to the Sirdárs of Kandahár, those Princes, as well as the Amír of Kábul, would be only the vassals of Persia, whilst the Sháh himself would be but an instrument in the hands of Russia, to be used, or not, as occasion might require, in direct hostility to our Indian Empire. A due regard even for the security of British India, to say nothing of the character which we have hitherto maintained in the regions bordering on our North-Western frontier, makes it indispensable that we should re-establish whatever influence and authority late occurrences may have deprived us of in Afghánistán.

'16. We have hitherto declined to take part in the intestine dissensions of the Afghán States, and when Sháh Shujá-ul-Mulk recently endeavoured to recover his throne, and advanced against the present ruler of Kábul, we gave no assistance either to that chieftain or to his antagonist. But as our efforts to cultivate a closer alliance with Dost Muhammad and his brothers of Kandahár have not only failed, but those Princes have, as it were, thrown themselves into the arms of a Power whose nearer approach to the Indus is incompatible with the safety of Her Majesty's Indian possessions, it becomes our imperative duty to adopt some course of

policy by which Kábul and Kandahár may be united
under a sovereign bound by every tie of interest as well
as gratitude to become, and to remain, the faithful ally
of Great Britain.

' 17. Such a prince might, we are inclined to believe, be
found in the person of Sháh Shujá, and we are disposed to
concur in the opinion offered to your notice by your Political
Agent at Ludhiána in his letter of January 1, 1838, addressed
to the Secretary of your Government. The inference to be
drawn from that letter seems to be that it would require but
a comparatively insignificant effort to replace Sháh Shujá
on the throne of Kábul and Kandahár, and that such a
measure would afford the best chance of rescuing that
important region from the arms of Persia and the arts of
her ally.

' 18. If, however, any effort so decisive is to be made,
means should be adopted to prevent almost the possibility
of failure. A considerable force, composed partly of British
troops, should be assembled on your North-West frontier, and
the Ruler of the Punjab and the Amírs of Sind invited to
co-operate with you. The countenance which the Mahárájá and the Amírs of Sind have already given to the
pretensions of Sháh Shujá, together with the advantages
which you might fairly offer to them by that alliance, would
induce Ranjít Singh and the Amírs to adopt your views;
and the Afgháns themselves, although naturally jealous of
the interference of the Sikhs in their internal concerns,
would not feel towards them the same hostility if they
appeared only as confederates of a British force.

' 19. An army so composed, properly equipped and prepared for an advance into Afghánistán, might be assembled
at any point most convenient, and, if you deemed it advisable
to make one more attempt to conciliate and secure the alliance
of the Chiefs of Kábul and Kandahár, you might dispatch an

officer of rank to each of those Princes, conveying to them
your final demands; and, in case the Sháh of Persia should
be in possession of Herát, or should still be engaged in the
siege of that city, a notification of the probable advance of
the British force into Afghánistán, and the objects of it,
might be also conveyed to that sovereign.

' 20. But immediate compliance should be required from
Dost Muhammad Khán and his brothers of Kandahár, and,
in case of refusal, the army should cross the frontier without
delay.

' 22. You should, moreover, declare your fixed determination to maintain the integrity and independence of the
restored monarchy against all encroachments of whatever
Power, and during the progress, and after the accomplishment of your enterprise, all your measures should have
a manifest tendency to accomplish that design.

* * * * * * *

' 26. We are aware that we have recommended to you
a course of policy and a series of measures which may require
great exertions, and entail upon your revenues sacrifices
only to be justified by the difficulties of your position. We
are also aware that in carrying our arms beyond the Indus
we may appear to contemplate schemes of aggrandizement
which every consideration both of justice and policy would
induce us to condemn. But, in truth, there is nothing
aggressive in that which we propose. The same wise pre-
caution which prompted your recent proceedings in Sind,
and the measures now in progress for opening and securing
the navigation of the Indus, dictates also the establishment
of a permanent British influence in Afghánistán.

' 29. The retreat of the Sháh from Herát, a renewal of
friendly relations between him and the British Minister, and
full reparation for the indignities of which Mr. McNeill has
complained, may render these measures unnecessary; but

even in that case you would do well to lose no time in
attempting to recover your influence in Afghánistán, and
to establish your relations with the Chiefs of that country
upon a more satisfactory basis than you have hitherto been
able to obtain.'

When, in 1851, Sir John Kaye published his
History, he held no appointment in Leadenhall Street.
But in 1857, and in 1874, when his second and third
editions were published, he was employed in the
Political Department, first of the Company, and later
of the India Office. He had gained access in those
years to all their political records. There was no
despatch so secret but he could lay his hands on it.
In his first edition he had made, on three occasions,
passing allusion in vague terms to despatches written
to Lord Auckland. But he had not attempted to consider their relation, in point of time, to the sequence
and development of events. Their effect on Lord
Auckland's policy had been represented as only one
of many factors ; and entirely secondary to an influence
which Sir John Kaye treated as supreme. Whatever
may have been his reasons (and it is idle now to
speculate upon them), he made no use whatever, in
1857 or in 1874, of the material which had become
available to him. In those later years, with the best
sources of information before him, he still preferred
mainly to attribute the policy of Lord Auckland to the
conjectured influence of his Indian advisers. In 1851
he had advanced, and in 1857 and 1874 he adhered
to, his theory of the Three Secretaries. These three

Secretaries, especially Colvin and Torrens, were so 'ardent and impulsive,' so 'bold and ambitious.' 'The direct influence mainly emanated from John Colvin.' Lord Auckland, separated from his Council, with whom had he remained he would never have decided on war, yielded, good, easy man, to 'the assaults of his scribes.' 'To what extent their bolder speculations wrought upon the plastic mind of Lord Auckland,' writes this careful chronicler, 'it is not easy with due historical accuracy to determine.' Anyhow, that which the Cabinet instructions of 1836 could not effect, neither the fears of McNeill, the desire of Hobhouse, the craft of Palmerston, *neque Tydides, nec Larisseus Achilles*, was conceded by Lord Auckland to 'three scribes.' The Persian host and Count Simonich at Herát, Witkewitsch at Kábul, the repulse of the British Agent from Kábul, the dismissal from Kandahár of a British officer, the scorn of Dost Muhammad, the agitation of all India, were considerations beneath serious attention. We have seen in our own time what response has been given from India to Russian intrigue in Afghánistán, and to the presence of a Russian envoy in Kábul. Lord Auckland, left to his own judgment, would have exclaimed with Banquo, 'The earth hath bubbles as the water has, and these are of them!' He might have prattled, had he been in the arms of his Council, about British Nervousness and Russian Herattitude. 'Macnaghten, Colvin, Torrens; Torrens, Colvin, Macnaghten:' the changes are rung and re-

I

rung on these names, and that is the tune the whole song goes to. Beyond surmise, Sir John Kaye admits that he has no authority. His sources are 'general conjecture,' 'well-credited report,' his own 'deliberate conviction,' the belief of one, the hint of another, the gossip of a third, for which, even as he transcribes it, he hastens to add that he will not vouch. He only repeats what is told him. 'Due historical accuracy' he will not lay claim to. Since the day of Herodotus was history ever so written?

Once he gives his authority. He writes that 'on the departure of the mission for Ludhiána' (July 13) that is, when Mr. Macnaghten left Ranjít Singh to present himself before Sháh Shujá, 'Burnes had proceeded to join Lord Auckland and his advisers at Simla.' If he did, it was contrary to Lord Auckland's expectations; who looked for him, as has been seen, with Mr. Macnaghten on July 17 or 18. Then he copies into his pages the following anecdote. The story is related in his *Narrative of Various Journeys*, by Mr. Masson. Dr. Buist, author of *Outlines of the Operations in Sind and Afghanistan*, repeated the story, adding that Masson was 'not a very trustworthy authority.' Sir John Kaye omitting this caution, prints the anecdote; though he admits that he was for a long time very sceptical of its truth, and does not even now vouch for it. But some men, he says, likely to be better informed, 'are inclined to believe it.' It has been questionable to the writer of this narrative, whether notice should be taken of a vagabond tale so fathered. But as it has passed into circulation with Sir John Kaye's book, a word may be devoted to it.

Captain Burnes, it is alleged, told Mr. Masson that the expedition across the Indus 'had been arranged before he reached Simla,' and 'that when he arrived Torrens and Colvin came running to him, and prayed him to say nothing to unsettle his lordship; that they had all the trouble in the world to get him into the business, and that even now he would be glad to retire from it.'

Now, apart from what has been shown in these pages to have been the actual course of events, the expedition across the Indus had not been arranged before Captain Burnes reached Simla, because we have it on Lord Auckland's authority that, till he saw Mr. Macnaghten (who, as Sir John Kaye says, did not reach Simla before Captain Burnes), he would settle nothing. We know that, rightly or wrongly, little store was set by Lord Auckland on Captain Burnes' judgment. Dr. Buist's book, with its disparaging remark on Mr. Masson, was before Sir John Kaye when he wrote; for he refers to Dr. Buist in the preface to his first edition. Sir John Kaye himself will not vouch for the story. Yet, gross as the calumny must be, if the story is proved untrue, he does not hesitate to reproduce it. Mr. Torrens gave it prompt contradiction. Mr. Colvin, to his last hour, never opened his lips on any one matter which had passed through his hands while he held the post of Private

Secretary. No man who has held such office, is at liberty publicly to discuss confidential matters which have relation to the discharge of his former duties. But the man who knows this, also knows that while he holds his office he is still less at liberty to tamper with sources of information to which his chief may address himself. The action attributed to Mr. Colvin may have seemed venial to those who made it their business to circulate the tale. In his own eyes, as in the eyes of all who have preceded or have succeeded him in the post which he then occupied, it would have been an act of unpardonable treachery. Sir John Kaye was wise in declining to vouch for the truth of a story which carries disproof on the face of it. But he exposes the absurdity of his hypothesis when he admits that his only positive evidence is evidence which he himself will not vouch for.

Before parting company with Mr. Masson, correction must be made of an attempt made by him to discredit the devoted and brilliant Chief Secretary who was to forfeit his life for his convictions. Mr. Macnaghten, it had been decided, should accompany the expedition as envoy. 'Mr. Macnaghten,' says Mr. Masson, 'volunteered his services for the occasion, on the ground that Burnes could hardly be depended upon in so important an affair.' Then he goes on to jeer and flout at Macnaghten in words which need not be transcribed. The truth is that on May 26, when on his way to Adínanagar, Mr. Macnaghten, in a letter before the present writer, proposed to Lord

Auckland that Colonel Pottinger, the agent at Haidarábád in Sind, should be the officer selected to accompany Sháh Shujá as British representative. It is very clear from the Diary that there was never at any time any question whatever of Burnes, who wrote, in fact, to ask for furlough because he had not been offered high political employment. The next day (July 30) he withdrew his letter; but eighteen days earlier, on July 12, Mr. Colvin had written by Lord Auckland's orders to Mr. Macnaghten in the following words :—

'It is right to let you know, that a strong feeling is grow- ing up here that it will be most desirable for the public interests, at whatever sacrifice to the daily case and satis- faction of Lord Auckland's administration, that you should assume the diplomatic direction of Sháh Shujá's expedition. The stake is so important that Lord Auckland feels that it may not become him to withhold his best card. Colonel Pottinger might in some respects do well. But (setting aside the possible objection on the score of his hard temper) he wants that general influence which is most essential. There must be free and confidential communication with the Government ; and besides this, influence at Lahore, influence at Peshāwar, over Wade, over Burnes, over every officer engaged, as well as thorough cordiality in Lord Auckland's views regarding Sind. All this it is not easy to see how to combine except in yourself. Think over this, and let me be aware as fully as you like of your own inclinations and opinions.'

Mr. Masson's assertion seems to have misled others. In his valuable fragment on *The First Afghán War*, the late Sir Henry Durand, who, taking a different tone from that of Dr. Buist, writes of Mr. Masson's 'truthful simplicity,' falls, possibly on Mr. Masson's authority, into the error that 'Mr. Macnaghten's proposal of himself as envoy met with the acceptance of the Governor-General.'

With the arrival of the cold weather of 1838 Mr. Colvin accompanied Lord Auckland to a great ceremonial gathering at Lahore, leaving Simla on November 7. On December 12 the party are at Amritsar. On December 18 he writes wearily in his Diary, 'a man of business tries in vain to be a student in tents.' On December 21 Lahore is reached; and among endless salutes, processions, festivities, and formal exchange of visits, his books are for weeks laid aside to make room for questions of precedence, Commissariat calculations, questions of tenure in the North-West Provinces, estimates of the cost of the late North-West famine,(which is put at 13½ lakhs, with 29½ lakhs of land revenue suspended, 'for eventual remission, no doubt'), Sátára claims, Nepálese and Burmese ambitions, and a hundred questions of the moment. On December 24 Sir Willoughby Cotton sends up the deposition of one Kásim Khán, a Kábul fruit dealer, who represents Dost Muhammad Khán as highly popular, and the restoration of Sháh Shujá as not at all desired. Mr. McNeill writes from Teherán in great delight at the October Proclamation. The army, meanwhile, is struggling on towards Kandahár and Kábul. On March 15 Mr. Colvin is again at Simla for the summer of 1839, and on April 5, Friday, he sees 'at last a prospect of returning rest, and brief regular periods of study :' with the results of which diary and commonplace book speedily run over. The summer passes, and he contemplates furlough. IIc has been thirteen years in India, and incessant labour is telling on him. Ghazní falls ; honours are recommended for Keane, Macnaghten, Pottinger, Wade, Sale, Thomson. Keane writes from Kábul that ' the feeling towards Sháh Shujá is not yet of a warm nature ;' Cotton, that ' the people of Kábul and its vicinity are much gratified by the change of rulers. But the Afgháns are a violent and treacherous people, and the Envoy has his work cut out for him.' On October 30 the Private Secretary leaves Simla ; and at Agra in the end of December, 1839, resolves to take furlough. Lord Auckland had decided to remain up country at Agra throughout 1840, and to administer the North-West, Mr. Robertson having declined the Lieutenant-Governorship. Suddenly all is changed. Events in China compel Lord Auckland's presence in Calcutta ; Mr. Robertson under pressure changes his mind, and takes the North-West ; the Governor-General hurries down, and his Private Secretary decides to stay on with his master.

He was to remain in Calcutta till March, 1842. The latter months of his residence were to be clouded by disasters in Kábul, by the murder of his friend Macnaghten, and by the distress of the Governor-General, with whom, in defeat as in success, he had passionately identified himself. This is not, it has been said,

a history of the Afghán war. It is a narrative only
of the events and discussions which preceded it. One
incident, however, calls for remark before quitting the
troubled scene of the Afghán imbroglio, because the
Private Secretary's good faith might possibly seem to
have been impugned in connexion with it. In the
end of 1840 the anxieties felt by the Ministry had
been echoed to Calcutta by the Board of Control. Sir
John Hobhouse sent a despatch to Lord Auckland,
urging him either to withdraw from Kábul, or to
strengthen his force there. For reasons which do not
concern this narrative, Lord Auckland contested this
counsel. It had by that time become clear to most
men that the central figure in the tripartite treaty
had completely failed in his share of it. Sháh Shujá
was a broken reed. He had no influence in Kábul.
On that vital point, all on whose information Lord
Auckland most relied, Burnes, Wade, Masson, Lord,
had, without exception, misled him. Dost Muhammad,
on the other hand, had given himself up voluntarily to
the British Envoy, and was in honourable captivity in
British India. The Mahárájá Ranjít Singh, his im-
placable enemy, was dead. In these later days the
question cannot but arise, whether terms might not
have been made, in 1841, with Dost Muhammad.
Would it not have been possible to recall Sháh Shujá
to honourable asylum at Ludhiána? Would Dost
Muhammad, in his fallen fortunes, have made in
1841, as in 1838, a *sine quâ non* of Pesháwar? Of
his influence in Kábul there was now ample proof.

Ultimately the Amír, as we all know, was sent back by
Lord Auckland's successor to Kábul, without conditions; and Sháh Shujá was left to his fate. Had
Lord Auckland profited by the occasion of the Board
of Control's despatch to make terms with Dost Muhammad, would not all his aims have been attained?

However, for reasons which it it not necessary here
to explain, this course approved itself neither to Lord
Auckland nor to his Council. They were unanimous
for prolonging the occupation of Kábul. A brief
despatch was sent to England to that effect, accompanied by three Minutes. Of these, one was by the
Governor-General, one by Mr. Prinsep, and one by
Mr. Wilberforce Bird. 'The question came before
the Council at the end of March,' says Sir John
Kaye in his *History*; 'either by some negligence, or
by some juggle, the opinions of the military members
of Council were not obtained. Lord Auckland and
the civilians decided in favour of the continuous
occupation of the country, though it was certain that
it could only be done at the cost of a million and
a quarter a year.'

In later years, at least, Sir John Kaye had at his
disposal the records of the East India Office; among
them the despatch in reply to Sir John Hobhouse,
dated March 22, 1841, of which the entire text is as
follows:—

'With reference to your Honourable Committee's despatch
of December 31 last, on the subject of our position and
policy in Afghánistán, we have the honour to forward, for

the information of your Honourable Committee, the accompanying copies of Minutes recorded on the subject by the Governor-General and the Honourable Messrs. Bird and Prinsep.

'2. The perusal of these will most fully explain to your Honourable Committee our views and sentiments in regard to the important question reviewed in your despatch above referred to.

'We have the honour to be, with the greatest respect, Honourable Sirs,

Your most faithful humble' servants,

AUCKLAND.
J. NICHOLLS.
W. W. BIRD.
WILLIAM CASEMENT.
H. T. PRINSEP.'

The military members of Council were Sir Jasper Nicholls, the Commander-in-Chief, and Sir William Casement, his colleague in the military department. The papers may not have reached the military members in time to admit of their recording Minutes. But the concurrence of all the members collectively in the Minutes sent home was unreservedly expressed in the despatch itself; 'the perusal of these will most fully explain *our* views and sentiments.' There is no qualification whatever, no syllable of dissent. If words have any meaning, the words of this brief despatch commit every member of Council who signed it to agreement with the views of the Governor-General.

Sir John Kaye, in support of his statement, quotes

a passage from Sir Jasper Nicholls' *Journal.* The asterisks are in Sir John's pages.

'March 26. Lord Auckland sent home a long Minute regarding Herát. * * * He means to preserve our footing in Afghánistán. Mr. Bird and Mr. Prinsep approve of this, though the latter roundly and justly asserts that it cannot be done under a crore and a quarter (a million and a quarter) annually ; and that no present mode of extending our receipts to that extent is open to us. Lord Auckland wrote a note to ask our opinions on the subject. Mr. Maddock never circulated the note. Sir W. Casement and myself were therefore silent.'

Whatever the object of this 'note,' or the subject on which 'our opinions were asked' may have been, they are immaterial to Sir John Kaye's statement, which is that Lord Auckland and the civilians alone decided in favour of the occupation of the country. The despatch of March 22, beyond all possibility of doubt, disproves this statement. Though the two military members did not record their opinions separately they expressed full concurrence in the views of their colleagues. Their opinions were to be found in the Minutes accompanying the Despatch.

In those last days of gloom and disaster it must have given pleasure to Mr. Colvin to receive, at a dinner given him by all his fellow-civilians in Calcutta, the warm tribute of their regard and affection. One of these on a subsequent public occasion, said of him:—

'Through six years he was the channel of approach to the Governor-General. It was through him that favours were

won, and through him that frowns descended.   I have
heard some who came away from his presence complain that
when he bowed, he did not bow low enough ; and some, that
he held his head a little too high.'   (It was in those years
that he got the sobriquet of ' King John,' which he retained
through the rest of his life.)   ' But I never heard any one
complain that he had been beguiled with honied words, or
with promises which were not to be performed.   I never
heard any one impugn his honour, his fairness, his integrity,
his resolution to do what was right and just in every case
and under all circumstances.'

Lord Auckland spoke for himself. On February 28,
he adopted the unusual course of recording a Minute,
which he desired should be transmitted to the Court
of Directors, ' upon the services rendered to me, and
through me to the State ' by his Private Secretary.
The Governor-General's Private Secretary holds an
employment, he added, of very great labour, of very
delicate duties, and of implicit confidence, in all that
regards even the most important and secret interests
of the State.

' Mr. Colvin,' he went on, ' has worked, I may say rather
with me than under me, during six years.   He has had, as
he deserved, my entire confidence.   He brought to his duties
an extensive and accurate knowledge of the interests of
India, of its history, and of the details of its administration.
This knowledge has been greatly increased, particularly in
regard to our political relations ; and if the merit of having
brought forward from time to time subjects of difficulty
with clearness and regularity before the Council should ever
be ascribed to me, it could not be so with justice unless
acknowledgement were also made, as I am ready to make it,

of the industry, the research, the correctness of judgment, the accuracy of information, and the readiness in composition with which Mr. Colvin has assisted me. I may add, that in the secondary but important duty of forming a judgment on the character of public men, and in the distribution of patronage, I write with equal satisfaction of the faithful and efficient aid which I have found; and though it could not be but that offence and dissent in this branch of duty should occasionally have been excited, yet I cannot but feel that it is due to the tact and discrimination with which Mr. Colvin has performed his part in this branch of the administration, that so little of discontent has been exhibited upon it, and that its fairness has been pretty generally admitted.'

This Minute discriminates the value of the character of the work done for Lord Auckland by his Private Secretary. It is not the language of a man who, when disaster overtakes him, recognises that he has trusted too much to the subordinate of whom he is writing. There is a measure and a reserve in the phrases used which indicate that the limits, within which Mr. Colvin had served his chief, were marked in the writer's mind with precision. A little later, on reaching England, Lord Auckland wrote again :—

'In the very few instances in which shades of difference have ever occurred between us, I can remember nothing but such a habit of manly frankness as could alone make counsel useful; and I can never forget how hardly, how ably, and how faithfully you have laboured for me. I bear a most grateful recollection of the infinite use which I have derived from these labours.'

On March 12, 1842, at half-past six in the morning,
the great hall at Government House is again thrown
open, as on that 21st day of October in 1837, when the
Misses Eden came down to take their coffee. The
Bishop, the Chief Justice, the Councillors are all
there. The same scene, with needful variations, is
enacted; and, at about seven, the procession again
moves on foot to Chandpál Ghát, 'followed by the
Body-Guard.' It passes through a double row of
soldiers, 'composed of H. M. 62nd and the 6th Madras
Native Infantry,' from the north-west gate of Government House to the Strand. On the Strand there is
a great concourse. The soldiery, for the last time,
present arms; his lordship, 'under strong emotion,'
returns the salute. He steps into a state barge; ap-
plies to his eyes, as a local reporter puts it, ' the handkerchief,' (as though there were a state handkerchief,
like a state barge or state elephants), and is rowed
out into the river to the *Lord Hungerford*. 'The
moisture in his eyes was visible,' writes an observer;
they are *lacrymae rerum*, wrung from him by mortal
suffering. No Governor-General ever left India with
a greater burden on his shoulders; but it was
lightened for him by the sympathy which surrounded him. It is plain from all contemporary
accounts that he was singularly beloved in India.
'He embarked at Chandpál Ghát,' said a Calcutta
paper, ' with the universal acknowledgement that he
had not left an enemy behind.' The patience and
dignity with which he had borne his misfortunes, his

gentle temper, his kindly nature, his large hospitality and unassuming carriage, had won him the hearts of all who met him. If he had failed, he had greatly ventured ; and to those who greatly venture in the cause of Great Britain, their countrymen in India forgive much. The malice with which his successor assailed his actions secured to him the sympathy even of those who judged his policy unfavourably.

CHAPTER VI

MR. COLVIN arrived in England with Lord Auckland
in August, his family having preceded him in January.
Sixteen years had passed in the East; and the ensuing
three and a half years were to give him the only
leisure of his lifetime. They passed, like all pleasure,
too rapidly. During the earlier part of this time he
was much engaged in helping Lord Auckland with
material to be used by his friends in Afghán debates
in the Lower House, or by the late Governor-General
in his own defence in the Lords. He wrote on the
same subject in the Whig organ, the *Morning
Chronicle*. Of the East India Company Directors
he saw much; of John Stuart Mill, then at work
in Leadenhall Street, not a little. Lord Auckland
presented him to many of his political friends. The
names of eminent men of the moment, now dropped
into obscurity, are frequent in his Diary. He renewed his acquaintance with Macaulay, his friendship
with Trevelyan. He read voraciously, adding largely
to the stock of information which he had laboriously
brought together in India. His two elder sons were

at Eton; the business of education (for younger brothers were pressing on their heels) commenced to occupy his attention. Few men have given more thought to their children, or lavished more on their bringing up.

He lived partly in London, where he had taken a house in Sussex Gardens; partly at Little Beal- ings in the neighbourhood of Ipswich, where his father had bought a property called 'The Grove'; partly at Purfleet and at Southill in Bedfordshire, where he was the guest of the late Mr. William Whitbread, who, in his second marriage, became the husband of Mrs. Colvin's widowed half-sister, Mrs. Macan. Two summers were spent in the Isle of Wight, Mrs. Colvin's birthplace. In September, 1843, he made a tour in Scotland, revisiting his old home at St. Andrews and other familiar haunts, and sending to his wife a diary of his experiences. A glimpse of this diary may be hazarded here, for it gives some sketch and description of that ancient city, as Mr. Colvin, who had known it from 1812 to 1821, again found it in 1843. St. Andrews, in 1843, boasted 'a direct coach to Edinburgh, as well as two to Dundee; a going ahead quite unthought of in my early time.' As no one had told him of these coaches, 'I came in the antique manner, by coach to Cupar from Edinburgh, thence to St. Andrews by post chaise. Yet the old way was the most propi- tious to my purpose. I passed all the well-known towns and marks; the road to Dundee so often

travelled when holidays came round; the narrow
Guard Brig, where, in my youth, resided the county
hangman, with his ancient endowment of four acres
of land; the golfing links and the rude narrow path-
way of stone over the "Swilken burn," under the
West Port, and along the wide quiet street to the
great hostelry of St. Andrews, the Black Bull Inn,
still managed by the family of Christies.' Black Bull
Inn and Christie have disappeared; and down that
wide, quiet street the last wheel alike of Edinburgh
and of Dundee coach has long since echoed away.

He goes over all the old scenes, to the schools, to
the University, to the belfry of the old parish church,
'where I was a great hand at helping to pull the
bells.' He finds the 'centre part of the main street
has been new paved; and the raised middle line of
stones, along which we youngsters, boys and girls,
were in the habit of running or rather jumping, has
long disappeared.' Even the 'reformed pavement is
now condemned. £500 of subscriptions have been
raised in the town, and there is to be a macadamized
centre street, with broad and flagged uniform pavement (London and Edinburgh fashion) on both sides.'
New sights and sounds everywhere greet him; for St.
Andrews had moved too; though in the St. Andrews
of 1894 he would have found changes little dreamed
of in 1843. 'At seven o'clock, boys and girls, the
former dressed with a smartness which has travelled
railroad pace from England, were moving in numbers
to the new Madras College.' He is reassured, however,

—for, after all, old things are the best—by 'the ancient plaster on many of the houses, black, brown, and chequered with time; the crumbling slates on many roofs; the general aspect of quiet desertion.' In the midst of these appears the incongruous figure of a Calcutta attorney. He passes on to 'the small wonder of St. Andrews; a neat new street of good moderate-sized houses, called Bell Street, which has arisen facing the golfing links.' At the Links he finds a Union Parlour 'for the convenience of golfers; and in its neighbourhood a number of small lodging-houses, which are also a new feature of St. Andrews.' This Union Parlour is a great sign of a new time, for 'in my days the golfing apparatus was kept in dirty, upstairs rooms of the golf caddies.' Now, in 1894, on the site of the Union Parlour, itself long superseded by a Club, is rising a monster, red brick hotel. He finds a monument in course of erection to the Scotch martyrs : pronounced by his companion, in Scotch phrase ' " a fulish thing." ' Necessarily he goes golfing; and walking round the oft-trodden course is 'strangely affected.' He breakfasts with Sir David Brewster, Principal of the University; meeting a young man, one Doctor Lyon Playfair, who is already rising into eminence. He hunts up Professor Haldane (of the profusion of capitals), now Principal of St. Mary's College. Presently he leaves St. Andrews, never to return to it; but, before he does so, he goes to see an old servant of his Uncle's, Peggy Anderson. ' I found her, such is the habit and ability

of the Scotch poor, writing a long letter, on foolscap
paper, to her son, a sailor in the Mediterranean. She
greeted me warmly, and amused me by coming out, after
many haltings and ha's, with "Aweel, Maister John,
your wife—how is she? She's na black is she, sir?" '

His furlough, like this visit, came too soon to an
end; and on Saturday, September 20, 1845, 'the
Liverpool left Southampton at 3 p.m.' He returned
alone to India, for he did not know what instructions
awaited him on arrival, or where he would have to
set up his home. Arriving in Calcutta on November 7,
he waited till January 8 before orders reached him
from Lord Hardinge to proceed to Khátmándu, and
to take charge of the Nepál Residency. In eight
days he had left Calcutta, and reaching Segaulí on
February 2, he arrived at his destination on February 8, with his old Haidarábád friend Ravenshaw, who from Patná had accompanied him. On
February 27 Ravenshaw returned, and he was left
to his new life. His predecessor had been Henry
Lawrence, who wrote to him shortly after he assumed
office in Nepál that the more the Rájá and the Durbar
were left to themselves the better. 'It was my
endeavour to bring matters back to Mr. Gardiner's
system (Mr. Gardiner had been · the first Resident
after the war of 1815); two visits a year, and half
a dozen letters to Government.' This was not the
kind of work which was likely to interest either the
man who wrote that advice, or the man to whom it
was given. Matters were ripening at the time for

the *coup d'état* which brought Jang Bahádur into prominence, and ultimately into power. But as yet there was no stir visible. The movements of the Resident at Khátmándu were—and still are—restricted almost within the grounds of the Residency. After having found himself in the centre of affairs when last in India, it was painful to Mr. Colvin to be relegated to the extreme verge of public life. The monotony of residence in Nepál was in sharp contrast too with the activity on the Sutlej, where the first Punjab War had begun. Either on his journey to Nepál, through forest and swamp-land, or while resident there, Mr. Colvin had contracted malaria. He fell seriously ill. His solitude aggravated his malady, which in turn reacted on his spirits. In June he was ordered away for change of air, returned to Calcutta, and in the close of the year, his wife having meanwhile rejoined him, he received orders to proceed to Maulmain, and to take charge as Commissioner of the Tenasserim Provinces on the Bay of Bengal. There he was to relieve Captain (later Sir Henry) Durand, of the Engineers.

Maulmain, when Mr. Colvin reached it on December 29, 1846, had recently lashed itself into a cyclone of fury. The story has been told in the life of Sir Henry Durand, by his son. The matter which had brought Captain Durand into collision with the Maulmain timber merchants, who formed the bulk of the local residents, was the recent course of forest administration. Tenasserim, with its valuable teak forests

on the Attaran, Thaung-yin, and Salwín rivers, had
been ceded to the East India Company in 1826.   At
first, the Attaran forests had been worked on Government account; but in May, 1829, the failure of the
experiment of cutting and exporting timber for the
Calcutta market had induced the Government to
throw open the forests under a code of rules to private
enterprise.   Licences wore given to cut timber to
a number of European and native speculators.   The
desire to profit by the trade in timber overruled all
considerations for the future.   The Maulmain timber
trade flourished; but the forests wero rapidly destroyed.   By 1840 the mischief had become so serious
as to lead, in the ensuing year, to revision of the rules
of 1829.   In 1841 a Superintendent of Forests was
appointed; but in 1846 Captain Guthrie, the Forest
Superintendent of that day, found that the rules were
still disregarded; and, with the support of Captain
Durand, the Commissioner, put in force certain measures
of repression.   These led to conflict between the administration and the merchants.   Resumption of the
licences which had been abused, and the substitution
of Government management for the licensing system,
formed the policy of the Commissioner; the Maulmain
merchants and the Calcutta press stormed against it.
Eventually it was disapproved by the Deputy Governor
in Calcutta, who, in the absence of Lord Hardinge,
the Governor-General, then in the Punjab, was the
authority before whom the question came.   Sir Her-
bert Maddock declared that it was not the intention

of the Government to monopolize the forests, to
restrain the free trader, or to trench on the rights of
grantees, or the lessees of forest lands. Mr. Colvin's
first business was to settle this forest question. In
1847 the estimated number of teak trees still remaining in the three forests is shown in a collec-
tion of papers relating to the Tenasserim forests,
published by the Government in 1862, to have been
as follows :—

Section.	Name of Forest.	Number of teak trees in occupied tracts.	Number of teak trees in unoccupied tracts.
1	Attaran	75,146	—
2	Attaran	—	18,392
3	Salwin	—	14,660
4	Haung-tharaw	—	2,014
5	Thaung-yin	—	83,970

In the third section, it would seem that there were
some lessees still in possession ; but, speaking generally, the disposal of the trees in the last four sections
was the matter which awaited Mr. Colvin's decision.
He regarded the orders of the Calcutta Government
as disposing of the first section, which having been
denuded of timber had practically disposed of itself.
Dr. Brandis (afterwards Sir Dietrich, and Inspector-
General of Forests in India), in a Report, dated 1860,
says in this regard, ' From this time (1845) the history
of the Attaran forests began in a great measure to lose
its practical interest, as regards the general welfare of

Maulmain. The supply of teak timber from these forests fell to less than 1000 tons per annum, other forests having taken their place. Mr. Colvin considered the lapse of the greater part of the Attaran forests as a *fait accompli*, which could not be altered.' He proposed, says Dr. Brandis, to retain for Government with one exception the large forests on the Attaran, for which no licences had yet been granted, and he arranged that extensive plantations should be established for the preservation of these forests, and for the renewal of timber from time to time removed from them. The Attaran licence holders in section 1 he was prepared to leave in possession; and of the unoccupied forests in section 2 to grant one lot to an European firm which had applied for it, reserving to Government the teak timber in the other lots of section 2, as well as the teak trees in sections 3, 4, and 5. For the forests retained under private licences he wished to give long leases, recommending the cession in perpetuity to the licence holders of all locations occupied by them. He was aware that holders in perpetuity might possibly not think it worth while to form plantations, or to provide for the growth of young trees, which could return no value till eighty years after they had been planted. But in his eyes, the question was not whether it was desirable to part with these forest lands to private persons—that was a *fait accompli*; the question was whether, having parted with them, it was not better that the transfer should be on the most sound terms.

Perpetual leases were not approved by the Court of Directors, who confirmed Mr. Colvin's other proposals, as well as the plantation experiments, and the direct administration of all tracts in the three sections reserved for Government. Dr. Brandis, writing twelve years after Mr. Colvin had left the province in 1848, and coinciding with his policy, proposed that while all other forests should be retained in direct management, all forests in section 2 should, like those in section 1, be made over to private enterprise. He recommended that the holders of existing licences in these forests should be called on to prove by their terms exclusive right to teak or other timber. He wrote :—

'India is not the country where the advantage of a provident management of forests is generally understood. The interests of a few persons only in this country reach beyond a limited number of years ; and this feeling of exclusive regard for the interests immediately before them easily communicates itself to public servants, as well as to private parties. We must, therefore, expect that, from time to time, violent outcries will be raised in India against the administration of forests by the Government. By proposing to leave the Attaran forests entirely in the hands of private parties, we give fair play to the other side ; and can afterwards draw comparison between the results of both systems. The Attaran forests, made over to private enterprise, will, it is hoped, prove the safety-valve for forest administration in India.'

Dr. Brandis' proposals were approved by the Government of India. 'The result was,' he has kindly informed the writer, 'that no claims or titles were proved to the satisfaction of the Committee appointed to examine, within six months, the authenticity of all permits or tithes. If I do not mistake, very few claims were brought forward at all. The fact was the Attaran forests had been exhausted, and presented no further interest to the holders. The greater part of the Attaran forests lapsed to Government, and they are now being managed in a proper systematic manner.'

But Mr. Colvin was not only the head of the executive Government in Tenasserim. He was also the chief judicial authority and local Court of Appeal. In this union of judicial and executive functions in one person, Tenasserim was administered on the lines of what came to be known, after the annexation of the Punjab in 1848, as the 'Non-Regulation' system. In attempting to improve the procedure of the Courts subordinate to him, in extending road communications, in problems of land revenue assessment, in regulating the many questions which surrounded the local timber traffic, and in an occasional dispute with neighbouring Burman authorities, Mr. Colvin found his time fully occupied. In the close of 1848, while engaged in these labours, he was summoned by Lord Dalhousie to Calcutta, to take his seat on the Bench of the Company's Chief Court of Appeal. To him the summons was probably not unwelcome; but the Maulmain community, in an address presented to him on his departure, expressed in

pleasant words their sense of regret at losing him.
Some of their sentiments may seem to have been
winged at his predecessor rather than addressed to
himself. They summed up his record in saying
that he had succeeded in his task of restoring order,
satisfying conflicting interests, reconciling party feelings, and establishing a healthy system of administration. Even the section of the local press which
. was in chronic opposition echoed the sentiments
of the address, and had nothing but genial words
as to Mr. Colvin's efforts to restore order and peace
where he had 'found the officers of Government ready
to fly at each other's throats on the least occasion,'
and where 'all were distracted with contentions.'
'Let us drop a mantle,' said the organ of opposition,
'over the few faults that were discernible.' The
mantle being duly dropped, in the last days of 1848
Mr. Colvin, followed by good wishes, crossed the Bay
of Bengal and once more set foot in Calcutta.

The Bengal public, it was afterwards said, were
somewhat astounded to hear that Mr. Colvin had been
appointed a Judge of the Sadr Court. 'The objections
to the appointment were many. With some, he had no
experience. With others, he had no temper. Again,
he had no knowledge of legal matters. But the
master who placed him there seldom made a mistake
in the selection of his agents.' The truth was that
the reputation of the judicial branch of the Civil
Service in Bengal had sunk below the level of the
executive branch. Ambitious and capable men found

more openings for distinction in the administrative line. The latter has always been the more popular. There is greater freedom of action about it. Its duties are more varied. Life is spent much on tour among the people. Sport can be freely indulged in. The prizes are more considerable. When Mr. Colvin took his seat on the Calcutta Bench he brought with him little experience of law beyond what he had gained at Maulmain. Before he left it, less than five years later, he had become, said Sir Charles Trevelyan in his Memoir of his friend, '*facile princeps*; so much so that it was commonly said that the pleaders had to be sometimes reminded that they ought to address the Court and not Mr. Colvin.' The Calcutta Sadr when he joined it had a questionable reputation. Barristers who ventured across the Maidán from the Supreme Court came back with strange tales of the quality of justice administered at Alípur; of antiquated procedure; of misuse of evidence; of arguments misapprehended. Throughout his term of office, Mr. Colvin laboured successfully, not only to raise the Court to the level which a Chief Court of Appeal should occupy, but to improve the quality of all Courts subordinate to it. He especially aimed at raising the character of the native bar; and, it is to be noted that in 1857, after his death, a meeting held at Calcutta to do his memory honour was first convened by a native pleader, Rámapersad Ráo. The value of a judge's work is to be found in his judgments rather than in any record of administration.

But testimony was borne to his judicial capacity at the meeting referred to by two who were peculiarly qualified to give it, by Mr. Ritchie, then Advocate-General, and Sir James Colvile, afterwards Chief Justice. Bábu Rámapersad Ráo had said that Mr. Colvin 'had done more for the improvement of the East India Company's Courts, and for the administration of justice generally, than any judge who had gone before him.' Sir James Colvile referred to his eminence in the Court. Mr. Ritchie added—

' To what has been stated by my learned friend Rámapersad Ráo, respecting Mr. Colvin's career in the Sadr Court, I can bear most cordial and willing testimony. In that Court, Mr. Colvin brought to bear, with characteristic energy and with signal success, his ripened faculties, upon the improvement of the law, and the advancement of justice— a task new to him, but not the less vigorously performed. During the first year of his career as a judge, he perhaps leant, as was natural to one new to the science of law, in his desire to correct a laxity he thought prevalent, to rigour sometimes bordering on technicality, in the application of the regulations according to the letter and the strict practice of the Courts. But it was to his honour that after he became familiar with and master of his subject, he retraced his steps in that respect, cast off technicality, except for the legitimate purpose of protecting the suitor from fraud or chicane, and administered the law of his Court, according to the sound principles of justice, and to the spirit rather than the mere letter of the regulations so as to command the admiration of all impartial men.'

The years which he passed on the Calcutta Bench were possibly the happiest in his life. He was among

valued friends, by whom his attachment was fully
reciprocated. His health in the moist Calcutta climate
gave him none of that anxiety which many feel; his
wife and younger children were with him.   His two
elder sons had come out from Haileybury, and had
entered the Indian Civil Service.   In Hastings House
at Alípur, he extended to all his acquaintances a
wide and warm hospitality.   His reading had made
him an excellent companion; and he delighted in
converse with the best and ablest of those about
him.   Since 1842 he had been charged with no
duties adequate to his abilities.   At a bound, he had
made himself the first, almost the only authority on
the Bench of the chief Bengal Appellate Court of the
Company.   He must have felt that in recovering
public respect for the Court, and in securing for himself a conspicuous position in it, he had vindicated
the reputation formed in earlier years.   His thoughts,
doubtless, recurred often to old days; to Macaulay's
breakfast parties, to morning rides with Trevelyan,
and, most of all, to long hours spent within the walls
of Government House, in the service of the kind chief,
whose sudden death on New Year's day, 1849, cast
a shadow over Mr. Colvin's return to the capital.

CHAPTER VII

LIEUTENANT-GOVERNOR, NORTH-WEST PROVINCES, 1853-1857

ON September 27, 1853, Mr. Thomason, Lieutenant-Governor of the North-West Provinces, died; and within a few days of the news reaching Calcutta, Mr. Colvin was again picked out by Lord Dalhousie, and selected as Mr. Thomason's successor. The appointment was received with general approval. The feeling found expression in the columns of one of the leading newspapers, when it said that 'Mr. Colvin will meet those whose actions he goes to direct, bearing with him the seal of the admiration of his former associates in Calcutta.' His brother civilians entertained him on October 25, at a cordial dinner at the Town Hall; and a day or two later he left Calcutta for the last time, twenty-seven years after he had first entered it. On November 3, 1853, he took charge at Benares of his new duties.

The North-West Provinces were not unfamiliar to him. During 1838 and 1839, when Lord Auckland personally administered them, it has been seen that Mr. Colvin was in close and constant communication with Mr. Thomason, then the Secretary to the

Government at Agra. He had marched through much of them; had learned not a little of their circumstances and needs; had personally become acquainted with the various classes by whom they were inhabited, with their agricultural tenures, and with the character of their great cities. He knew many of the leading officers; and to all his name and antecedents were familiar.

Since 1853 the limits and the jurisdiction of the North-West Government have been greatly changed. Subsequently to 1857, considerable tracts, which up to that date had been under the Lieutenant-Governor, were transferred to other administrations. In 1876 Oudh was added to his charge. In 1853 the Province comprised fifty-one districts, with a population of about 35,000,000, the majority being Hindus, mixed with a large and powerful Musalmán element. It occupied an area of nearly 120,000 square miles, and numbered about 100,000 townships or villages, contributing to the revenues of India little less than £6,000,000 sterling. It extended from a point on the Sutlej to the frontier of the Bombay district of Khándesh; and from Nímach in the heart of the Rajwára States to the boundary of Nepál. In the superintendence of the judicial affairs the Lieutenant-Governor was assisted by a Chief Court of Appeal, corresponding to the Sadr Court of Bengal in Calcutta, where Mr. Colvin had recently sat. Revenue matters were administered under his authority by a Land Revenue Board. In certain outlying tracts the land revenue administration was exercised by the Agents to the Governor-General in Rájputána and Central India, in subordination to the Lieutenant-Governor. The unit of administration was the District, which was usually an area of 1,100 or 1,200 square miles, presided over by an English 'Magistrate and Collector,' answering to a French *sous-préfet*; the *Préfet* being the 'Commissioner,' under whom were grouped five or six districts.

Within the area of the North-West Province is comprised all that is most national and most sacred in the sight of Hindus; much that reminds Muhammadans of the past glories of the Mughal empire is to be found also within its limits. In the south-east rise the spires of the innumerable temples of Benares, the bourne of every Hindu's desire, and the goal of his frequent pilgrimages. Not far from Benares is Prág, known better by its Muhammadan name of Allahábád, situated at the junction of the Ganges, the Jumna, and the fabled Saraswatí, a spot little less sacred than Benares; and, like Benares, the desire of countless pilgrims. In both cities swarm devotees, priests, ascetics, all the hierarchy of the Hindu religious fraternities. From west to east of the Province flow the sacred Ganges and Jumna, issuing each from its couch of snows on glittering Himálayan peaks. Muttra and Brindában feed the flame of Hindu devotion, enshrining in their temples the figure of incarnate Vishnu, known to man as Ráma and as Krishna, whose victories live in the songs, as his name reigns

in the hearts of the people. Nor to the Muhammadan
is the Province less instinct with heart-stirring
traditions. To him the North-West Provinces, as
they existed in 1853, were identical with his own
' Hindustán.' All the might of the Mughal had been
centred in it. The imperial cities of Delhi and Agra
were its boast. To their Halls of Audience had flocked
suppliants from every Court in India; the rude
Turkoman from Central Asian steppes; the polished
Persian of Isfahán; the swarthy Nubian from the
Nile; the pale Christian from across the further seas.
The royal palaces of Agra and Delhi were monuments
worthy of the proud dynasty which had erected them.
Within the walls of the Delhi fort—a shadow of the
glories of his great house, but yet a name to conjure
with—lingered the aged Emperor. The Company
was a cold abstraction, towards which it was impossible that loyalty could be felt. But to the
heart of every Muhammadan in Upper India the
despised and pensioned Mughal pleaded powerfully in
his obscurity.

The races which swarmed within the Province were
little likely to be deaf either to priest or Emperor.
In the public offices, in social life, in the ranks of the
army, the Bráhman asserted, and, indeed, had been
encouraged by the Company in maintaining, his pre-
eminence. The Rájput rivalled him in pride, and,
in audacity, surpassed him. Restless tribes of pre-
datory type crowded upon the land, at frequent feud
amongst themselves, and ever ready for collision

with the authorities. The Gujar, the Mewáti, the Rángar, the Ahír, were all elements of unrest, and of upheaval. Shekh, Sayyid, Mughal, Pathán, tracing their origin from every country where the Fátiha is recited, contrasted the daily drudgery of the plough with the fortunes and the fabled successes of their ancestors. These, with their strong right hands, had carved out the patrimony from which their children, in the sweat of their brow, in increasing numbers wrung a dwindling pittance. Remembrance of the past embittered the actual hour. From the gates of the crumbling fort, through which the Pathán now hastened in the chill morning to pay homage in the camp of the young Magistrate, had issued at dawn, within men's memory, fierce horsemen of that race who had swept the country from the Siwáliks to Delhi. Yet these, though in poverty, at least retained their lands. Others, not a few, who, at the commencement of British rule, had owned large estates, now found themselves ousted. The Province was full of dispossessed proprietors ; who, in the chances and changes of the first years of the Company's revenue administration, had been sold up in default of payment, or whose titles had been adjudged defective.

The Punjab had been rigorously disarmed, after its great national struggle. No such measure had been adopted in the North-West, which had come piecemeal, by cession or by conquest, at different epochs, under the Company's flag. It teemed with weapons. When, in 1859, after the Mutinies, systematic dis-

armament was resorted to, there were given up to
the authorities 795 pieces of ordnance, 307,372 fire-
arms, 1,421,223 swords, 664,015 spears, 1,215,275
daggers and other lethal weapons. Even then it was
calculated that 1,400,000 weapons of various kinds
remained unsurrendered. These were all in the hands
of the civil population throughout 1857 ; and to them
were added, during the disturbances, many fire-arms
and other weapons, the property of the Government.

For the last ten years, during Mr. Thomason's
government, the Province had been noted for the
vigour of its land revenue administration. Its officers,
trained in the school of Robert Merttins Bird, had
achieved eminent success. When the Punjab was
annexed, heavy drafts were made on the North-
West. Its best men, in their several grades, were
selected, and the Province was stripped of the flower
of its officers. 'When, in 1849, the administration of
the Punjab was freshly formed under the Lawrences,
many of the best and most rising men under Thomason
were taken by Lord Dalhousie for the new Province.
In private letters to Montgomery he writes thus of
his departed henchmen : "It has been a heavy tax.
Nineteen men of the best blood! I feel very weak
after so much depletion[1]."' Good men were left; but
the 'best blood' of the Province had been poured into
the Punjab four years before Mr. Colvin took charge
of it. When, a little later, the storm of the Mutinies
broke upon him, that loss, though it may have been

---

[1] *James Thomason*, by Sir Richard Temple, Bart., M.P., p. 101.

the vital gain of the one Province, was fatally felt in the other. The North-West was 'very weak after so much depletion.'

In the Punjab, too, were gathered the British bayonets. The flower of the military, as of the civil, service were in Lord Dalhousie's new Province. A Lieutenant-Governor is only a civil official. In extreme cases, the military secure order. In their efficiency is the last word of the administration. The distribution of the British and native military forces in April, 1857, three and a half years after Mr. Colvin took charge, was as shown in Table A, p. 166, in the North-West, in Oudh, and in the Punjab. Oudh was annexed in 1856, and the year 1857 is more convenient therefore than 1853 for the purpose of this comparison. The figures are taken from a return furnished to Parliament in February, 1858 ; and so much of the old Dinápur Division as lay in Bengal has been eliminated from them. The sick are not included, because the return does not discriminate between European and native sick.

The proportion of British to native troops in the Punjab, viz. 13,421 to 42,904, was, in round numbers, one to three ; in the North-West, with its 4,179 English and 41,410 native soldiers, one to ten ; in Oudh, where there were 993 English to 11,319 natives, one to eleven.

On May 1, 1893, the corresponding figures were as shown in Table B.

TABLE A.

Comparative strength and distribution of British and Indian troops in the North West Provinces, Oudh, and Punjab, 1856.

N.W. PROVINCES.		
Division.	ALL RANKS AND ARMS.	
	English.	*Native.*
Dinápur	489	6,701
Cawnpur	267	5,725
Saugor	327	10,627
Meerut	3,096	18,357
Total . .	4,179	41,410
OUDH.		
Oudh Field Force . .	993	11,319
PUNJAB.		
Sirhind	4,790	11,049
Lahore	4,018	15,939
Pesháwar	4,613	15,916
Total . .	13,421	42,904

TABLE B.

Comparative strength and distribution in 1893 of troops specified in Table A.

Provinces.	ALL RANKS AND ARMS.	
	English.	*Native.*
N. W. Provinces . .	12,897	15,929
Oudh	4,375	3,930
Punjab	20,515	42,360

The great arsenal of Delhi was in native hands. The North-West army was confided to veteran commanders; men of repute in their day, but now long past the vigour of their prime.

During his three and a half years of undisturbed rule, Mr. Colvin's efforts were directed mainly to three points—the improvement of the judiciary; reform in the police; and the resettlement of the Land Revenue of the Province. Before entering on his own work, it became his first duty to set the seal to the great enterprise which had long engaged his predecessor's attention. The Ganges Canal, schemes for which had as far back as 1838 been discussed with Lord Auckland, and which was first planned by Mr. Colvin's cousin, Colonel John Colvin of the Engineers, had been worked out and completed by Colonel Cautley and Major Baker of the same corps. The time had come in April, 1854, when the Canal was to be formally opened. It was hoped that Lord Dalhousie would be able to preside at the ceremony. But Lord Dalhousie had other affairs to attend to, and the duty devolved on his lieutenant.

Much at which Mr. Colvin laboured during the term of his Lieutenant-Governorship was cast into the furnace of 1857. From thence it re-issued, to be beaten out by the hands of his successors, but to take shape much as he had designed for it. His first aim was to strengthen the administration of the Courts which, in the North-West Provinces even more perhaps than in Bengal, had fallen into disesteem

The Revenue Department had absorbed all the most
capable men whom the Punjab had spared. The executive in India is apt at all times to be impatient of
the check exercised over it by the Bench, and it is
therefore of importance that the men in whose hands
such check is placed should be up to the level of
their business. Mr. Colvin found them to be otherwise, and devoted his first efforts to strengthening
the judiciary. He would not advance to the higher
executive posts men who had not served their time on
the Bench. He selected some of the best men whom he
could find in the Revenue branch, and sought to
transfer them to the Sadr Court. He deputed a judge
from that Court to visit each district, and to remedy
local defects. Incompetent judges were removed.
Officers, competent but too rooted in their charges,
were transferred. He tried especially to raise the
status of the lowest class of native civil judges, and
to secure the better training of men to fill subordinate
judicial posts. Anticipating one of the reforms which
was put into effect shortly after the Mutinies, he
asked from the Supreme Government the establishment of Small Cause Courts. He arranged for the
creation of the post of Government Advocate and
Legal Remembrancer. Since that day, the Sadr has
been amalgamated in the North-West with a High
Court established under Royal Charter. Macaulay's
Penal Code, after many years and much modification,
has become law. Admirable Codes of Criminal and
Civil Procedure have been enacted. The tone and

standard of the native judiciary has been steadily
raised. The quality of justice has been sensibly
improved. All, and more than all, that Mr. Colvin
worked for has been attained; but whatever has
been achieved has been on lines similar to those
which in his Administration Report for 1855-6 he
planned for observance.

So again, in the North-West Police Force, as it
was reorganized in 1863, and as it now exists, are
embodied many of the reforms for which Mr. Colvin
strove. He succeeded in reorganizing the staff of
Police Inspectors and Sub-Inspectors, so as to reduce
the number of the lower and proportionately to in-
crease the pay of the higher grades. To that end he
reduced considerably the number of Police stations,
bringing those that remained more easily under sur-
veillance. He invested the important class of native
Revenue Officers, who are employed, each in his own
subdivision, as Sub-Collectors under the English
Collector of the District, with some degree of authority and responsibility in Police matters. He established an official Police Gazette, in order to disseminate
quickly over the Provinces the news of heinous crimes,
and to strengthen a feeling of solidarity among the
force. He directed the distribution of Police duties
between the District Magistrate and his subordinates,
especially enforcing the personal responsibility of the
former in regard to the District Police administration. Vigorous measures were taken against organized
crime. Outlaws and professional gangs of robbers or

of murderers, such for example as Thugs, were hunted down with unwearying patience. Registers of habitual criminals were established in each district. Character books for the several members of the Police force were established. A small number of the force in each district were trained to the use of firearms for the purposes of escort and guard. A model was prescribed for police stations, 'so as to take away from them the character of enclosed buildings, removed from public observation,' and they were brought into the immediate vicinity of the sub-district Revenue offices. The mists of time have obscured the origin of much which is now familiar, in their Police system, to North-West district officers, and which many probably imagine to date from some period after the Mutinies. But, in the Report above referred to, all this and more will be found.

Road communications, elementary and higher education, jails, all the incidents of active internal administration passed under Mr. Colvin's scrutiny and review. Those were not days of decentralization; and it is instructive to see that the sanction of the Court of Directors had to be obtained before a branch of the Grand Trunk Road could be carried from Meerut to Rúrki at a cost of £22,000. Now the railway has in its turn superseded the Grand Trunk Road; and the great thoroughfare of 1855 has, in 1894, become obsolete. In railways Mr. Colvin took the keenest interest. What is now the East India Railway was in course of construction. We find him, in

1855, advocating a line identical with that which, now known to us as the Oudh and Rohilkhand Railway, traverses the latter Province, and urging construction of the railway which, by Baroda and Rájputána, at present links Bombay with Agra and Delhi.

In India, as in other Eastern countries, the State is, in theory, the landlord, and claims a share in the produce of the soil. In British India the theory has been modified, in compliance with Western ideas. But it has never been wholly abandoned. The Government has conferred (subject to payment of its land revenue) proprietary possession on various classes occupying the soil, contenting itself with claiming a share in the net rental. The annual cash value of such share is computed at recurring terms of thirty years, by the process of what are known as 'Settlements.' The proportion of the Government share has varied in different times and Provinces. When Mr. Colvin assumed office, the last Settlement of thirty years was expiring, and he had to lay down rules for the valuation of the thirty ensuing years' annual rental. The Government of the North-West hitherto had taken an annual share based on the computed value of sixty-six per cent. of the net rental assets. He fixed the proportion to be in future taken at fifty per cent. only. Practically, the proportion of sixty-six per cent. had been nominal. At the preceding period of valuation there had been much waste land not included in the estimate. This had been since brought into cultivation : and, during the

thirty years' term, its yield had become available to
the proprietors who broke it up. In many tracts
such lands had amounted to forty per cent. of the
whole cultivable area at the previous valuation; in
some cases to seventy per cent. Where the Government share of the rental assets, in the absence of
a cultivable margin or for other causes, had really continued throughout the thirty years' term at sixty-six
per cent. of the net rental, the burden had proved un-
bearable. Large reductions of the Government demand
had in such cases been found necessary. Much property had been mortgaged or sold. In 1854, no sufficient cultivable margin remained, to reduce, throughout the Province, during the ensuing term of thirty
years, a nominal sixty-six to an effective lower figure.
Mr. Colvin decided that, in future, not more than half
the net rental should be claimed by the Government
as its share. Local cesses for schools, roads, and so on,
have increased the amount payable in one or another
form by the proprietor. The ultimate net income of
the proprietor from the land is rarely above forty per
cent. of the net rental. Though Mr. Colvin's decision
has from time to time been assailed, experience has
confirmed its wisdom, and it continues the rule of
practice.

The note of his administration was vigour. Sir
Charles Trevelyan, in his paper in the *Times*, says
that his secretaries, who could scarcely keep abreast
of the work put upon them, complained that he over-
governed. Being new to the Province, he had to

acquire a great deal with which his predecessor, from his youth, had been familiar. Hence correspondence increased. He consulted his officers much ; forming them, for that purpose, into little groups, like Councils. Sir George Campbell, in his *Memoirs*, mentions having taken part in those deliberations. 'I found him a very large-minded man, and it was a great pleasure to work with him.' The Lieutenant-Governor, for his part, quickly detected Mr. Campbell's abilities ; and, when a vacancy occurred early in 1857, offered him the post of Secretary to his Government. It was accepted ; but the Mutinies prevented Mr. Campbell, then in the Punjab, from taking it up.

The idle or the incompetent may have thought Mr. Colvin a hard man. He left the widest discretion and gave the most unflagging support to those whom he believed to deserve it. Impartial to the claims of all, easy of access, frank in personal address, courteous in correspondence, thoughtful of others, unsparing of himself, he soon gained the confidence of his subordinates in his new Province. His temperament was judicial. He liked to weigh, to examine, and to decide—not tardily, for he was prompt—but after due discussion. Though grave and rather stern in demeanour, his natural kindliness of disposition secured him the goodwill of his officers.

CHAPTER VIII

THE MUTINIES: DEATH, 1857

IN the midst of these labours, the Mutinies of May, 1857, fell upon the Lieutenant-Governor. He was at Agra, alone, Mrs. Colvin having gone to Europe earlier in the year. The three preceding summers had been spent happily at Náini Tál, in the Himálayas, and Mr. Colvin believed himself to have taken office on the condition that his summers should be spent in the Hills. Later, this understanding was questioned; and in 1857 he was to remain in the plains. His family went to Europe; and at Agra, on May 11, the news of the outbreak at Meerut reached him.

It has been seen what were the circumstances of the Province of which, in 1853, he took charge, and what was the English force that held it. In May, 1857, in two important respects, its defensive condition was even worse. Oudh had been annexed in 1856. That Province was surrounded on three sides by the North-West. It was the chief recruiting ground of the Sepoy army. It was seething with suppressed rage, and ready to throw fuel fresh and fresh on any flame lit across its border. All told, there were not 1,000 British soldiers in Oudh. Again, in the North-West the chief British force, it has been shown, was in the Meerut division. At Meerut there was a regiment of Queen's dragoons, and of British infantry, with one troop and one company of artillery. These were sent at once to Delhi, to take part in the siege. The detachment at Cawnpur was locked up in its own defence. The Dinápur and Saugor detachments, insignificant in number, were distant and inaccessible. All that remained to Mr. Colvin wherewith to make head at Agra against 42,000 rebel soldiers, were a battery of six guns, the drivers being natives, and a new and raw English regiment on the Company's establishment, of 655 effective rank and file. Jekyll, in his letters, relates that the Mayor of Oxford apologized to Charles II for omitting a royal salute when the king entered that city. He had, he said, three excuses; the first, that he had no cannon. The king graciously dispensed with the other two. It is unnecessary to dwell on reasons which prevented Mr. Colvin from making head against the Mutiny. His first reason, like that of the Mayor of Oxford, was sufficient.

He was at once cut off from all communication with the Commander-in-Chief and with the Punjab. He endeavoured to utilise the Native Hindu States around him, and to enlist their sympathies against the Delhi Emperor. He made a bold use of their troops and contingents. On May 16 Lord Canning, struck by the tone and substance of his telegrams, 'thanked him sincerely for all that he had so admirably done, and for his stout heart.' On May 18

he placed the belt of districts round Delhi under
martial law. He strained every nerve to get touch
of Delhi. But, in a few days he found that he
could obtain no news of what was passing there.
On May 25 he writes that, 'we have nothing
from Meerut for a week. The difficulty of getting
messages through is inconceivable.' On May 29,
eighteen days after the news of the first outbreak
came to him, 'not a line has reached me,' he tells
Lord Canning, 'from the Commander-in-Chief since
the commencement of the disturbances.' 'The reason
why messages are not delivered,' he adds, 'is, that
the belief in our power is shaken, and men will not
run the risk of detection. On the whole there is
(its police force being dispersed) no support to the
Government.' On May 31 the two native regiments
at Agra are disarmed. In a day or two the group of
districts round Agra, such as Aligarh, Muttra (whence
his son Elliot narrowly escaped), and Etah, 'are in
a blaze of riot and carnage.'

'Etáwah has been reoccupied by the advance which
I directed of the Grenadier Regiment, Gwalior Contingent
Infantry, from Gwalior. Mynpoory has saved its treasure,
prisoners, and records, by the determined energy of Mr. John
Power, the Collector. . . . The country north of Meerut is at
the mercy of the most daring and criminal. . . . I wield but
the purest shadow of government.'

Appeals for aid reached him from his officers.
None could be given. District after district 'went,'
as the phrase ran. There were no troops, no police,

no friends. The whole country was armed and in uproar. Then came news of massacres of men, women, and children. At Agra he had a large European and Eurasian population, and a great fort, with an armoury, which it was necessary to guard. He could not therefore spare a British soldier. Every weapon which he laid hold of snapped in his hand. Native States and their contingents alike proved broken reeds. His powerlessness at the last overwhelmed his spirit. A week before he died he attributed his mortal illness to his utter impotence. Enforced inaction at such a time was literally death to him.

Contrast between the course of affairs in the North-West Provinces and in the Punjab is impossible, because their circumstances were wholly dissimilar. In the Punjab was a very considerable English army. The Province was disarmed. The Sikhs had but recently been subjected to crushing defeat. The best military and civil officers in all India were at the disposal of the Punjab Government. The Punjabi hated the Sepoy, Hindu or Muhammadan, and the Mutiny was a Sepoy revolt.

'Our people being without arms,' wrote Sir John Lawrence to Mr. Colvin on September 14 (five days after the eyes of him whom he addressed had closed on all earthly tumults)— 'Our people being without arms has been doubtless the main cause of our success. The Sikhs have a traditional hatred of Delhi, and most of the Muhammadans do not sympathize with His Imperial Majesty.'

Sir Robert Montgomery (Sir John's chief lieutenant) had written, at an earlier date to Mr. Raikes, in a letter before the present writer :—

'Our five rivers, with their ferries, give us a great advantage, as no Purbea (Hindustáni) can show his face without being instantly seized. If a Sepoy deserter or mutineer, he is tried on the spot, and hanged. The Sikhs hate them, and if a Regiment breaks and runs, the whole population is after them. The Sepoys are strangers in a strange land. They have no sympathy from the people, and are not protected or concealed.'

Reverse these words, and we have the situation in the North-West. Arms were in every man's hands. The Sepoy was in his own home. No one questioned him. All favoured or feared him. The population were his brothers. He numbered over 40,000. There were not 800 British troops, all told, available against him.

On three points, closer inquiry is due to Mr. Colvin's memory. It has been said that he failed to detect the true character of the Mutiny till long after it had become apparent to others in high places. He has been reproached with the issue on May 25 of a Proclamation, inviting Sepoys to surrender on terms which Lord Canning compelled him to withdraw. He has been charged with apathy in the conduct of affairs in Agra itself, with neglecting the provisioning of the Fort, and with causing much loss of property by harsh restrictions as to the amount to be taken into the Fort, when events drove the Christian population to its shelter. Criticism has been directed to one or two minor incidents which do not call for any notice in these pages.

As to the first point, it is beyond doubt that the three men on whom the storm broke, John Colvin, John Lawrence, and Henry Lawrence, looked to the immediate attack upon Delhi, to nip the Mutiny in the bud. ' Unless Delhi and its magazine are recovered,' wrote Sir John Lawrence on May 13 to the Commander-in-Chief, ' the insurrection will assuredly spread. . . . By decisive measures at once we should crush the mutineers, and give support to the well-affected or timid. Time in such matters seems to be everything.' On May 23 Sir John[1] 'still thinks that no real resistance at Delhi will be attempted. . . . My impression is that on the approach of our troops the mutineers will either disperse, or the people of the city rise and open their gates.' He even touches on the measures of military reform to be taken later. On May 27 Sir Henry wrote[2], ' In a few weeks, if not days, unless Delhi be in the interim captured, there will be one feeling throughout the army. . . . Once Delhi is recaptured, the game will again be in our hands.' 'A victory at Delhi is the secret of all effect,' wrote Mr. Colvin on the 25th. Two days before, he had written to Mr. Mangles, ' Everything depends on the Commander-in-Chief's attack.' All three counted on that, and on that only. But of

---

[1] *Life of Lord Lawrence,* by Bosworth Smith, vol. ii. pp. 15, 33.
[2] *Life of Sir Henry Lawrence,* vol. ii. p. 327.

the three Provincial rulers one only, John Lawrence, was in communication with the Commander-in-Chief. To Mr. Colvin and to Sir Henry Lawrence all to the North-West of Delhi was impenetrable silence. On May 17 General Anson had already written to Sir John Lawrence, telling him what was the prospect. Even on May 29, twelve days later, Mr. Colvin had not found it possible, as we have seen, to get a word from General Anson. On May 30 Sir Henry Lawrence, writing to Mr. Raikes, asks for 'an occasional line till Delhi is taken.' The measure of the delay in learning the truth, was the measure of the hopefulness of the Lawrences and Mr. Colvin. Sir John Lawrence learned it first of the three; but each as soon as it came to him fathomed the situation. On May 29 (his fiftieth birthday), opening a letter from Lord Canning to General Anson, Mr. Colvin first learned that the attack on Delhi must be delayed. From that day he had no illusions. He tells Lord Canning on that date that the only course now before the Government is a cold-weather campaign. There is no more idea in his mind of a speedy end to the outbreak.

The second point on which comment is necessary is Mr. Colvin's Proclamation of May 25. On May 22 the Lieutenant-Governor wrote to General Anson: 'I would treat the Mutiny, on the part of many engaged in it, as a miserable delusion. Murderers and ringleaders I would except; but to the common herd I would offer remission of this punishment through dismissal, and on their laying down their arms.' This also seems to have been the spirit of the policy which commended itself to Sir John Lawrence ; ' to act at once, to recall the disloyal to a sense of duty, to assure the wavering, and to strike with effect against those in revolt [1].' On May 24 the Lieutenant-Governor wired to Lord Canning that he had received from him a message for transmission to the Commander-in-Chief and to Sir John Lawrence. The contents of the message are not given in the Blue Book, but it referred evidently to the treatment of mutineers. Mr. Colvin, in acknowledging the message to the Governor-General, replied :—

' On the mode of dealing with the mutineers I would strenuously oppose general severity towards all. Such a course would, as we are unanimously convinced by a knowledge of the feeling of the people, acquired amongst them from a variety of sources, estrange the remainder of the army. Hope, I am firmly convinced, should be held out to all those who were not ringleaders or actively concerned in murder and violence. Many are in the rebels' ranks because they could not get away : many certainly thought we were tricking them out of their caste. A tone of general menace would, I am persuaded, be wrong. The Commander-in-Chief should, in my view, be authorized to act upon the above line of policy. I have ventured to detain the portion of your message to the Commander-in-Chief after the words "speedily at Delhi".'

Lord Canning replied on May 25 that Mr. Colvin had done right to stop the latter part of his message

---

[1] *Life of Lord Lawrence*, by Bosworth Smith, vol. ii. p. 22.

to the Commander-in-Chief. Menaces are quite unnecessary. Those for whom no severity could be too
great are—every man in arms resisting the Commander-in-Chief; every man who had taken part in
the murder of an European officer or other person;
every ringleader; generally, a distinction should be
drawn between regiments which murdered their
officers and those which did not. 'To men of the
latter, forbearance in the first instance and hope of
pardon, if they could show a claim to it, may be
extended.' A few hours before receiving Lord Canning's reply, Mr. Colvin sent to Lord Canning the
text of the following Proclamation which he had
that day issued. The event which led to it was
the sudden mutiny of a contingent of Gwalior cavalry,
the only horse which he had at his disposal. The
incident proved to him that, if others might be dis-
suaded from following their example, no time must
be lost in addressing them. On May 25 he had heard
not a word from the Commander-in-Chief, and he still
looked for the early recapture of Delhi. Animated
by this expectation, he hoped to lessen the number of
those who might be misled by the mutiny leaders :—

'Soldiers engaged in the late disturbances, who are desirous
of going to their own homes, and who give up their arms
at the nearest Government civil or military post, and retire
quietly, shall be permitted to do so unmolested.

'Many faithful soldiers have been driven into resistance
to Government only because they were in the ranks and
could not escape from them, and because they really thought
their feelings of religion and honour injured by the measures

of Government. This feeling was wholly a mistake, but it acted on men's minds. A Proclamation of the Governor-General now issued is perfectly explicit, and will remove all doubt on these points. Every evil-minded instigator in the disturbance, and those guilty of heinous crimes against private persons, shall be punished. All those who appear in arms against the Government, after this notification is known, shall be treated as open enemies.'

The English text of this Proclamation is obviously open to criticism. Though Mr. Colvin daily expected Delhi to fall, it had not as yet fallen ; and an appeal to the soldiery seemed premature to those unacquainted with his anticipations. The English version exempts from pardon only evil-minded instigators and those who had murdered private persons. What of those who had murdered officers ? This point was at once seized upon in Calcutta, where the paper was received with a howl of indignation. The press raved at it ; Lord Canning and his Council hastened to disavow it. Though approved in Upper India, in Calcutta it was condemned. To none there does it seem to have occurred that there might be misconception. Mr. Colvin's known character, his stout heart in the front of unparalleled difficulties, might have led to hesitation in judging him. Unfortunately, Lord Canning had no personal knowledge of Mr. Colvin. Jedburgh justice was dealt him. No explanation was asked for, or, when tendered, was admitted. Not till later, when it became known that Sir Henry Lawrence had adopted the Proclamation, and that the English rendering was misleading, did misgivings and doubts as to the justice of the censure on him suggest themselves to Calcutta. There is but a step from the Capitol to the Tarpeian. From the eminence which in thirty years he had achieved, Mr. Colvin fell in an instant into discredit.

Lord Canning's objections to the text of the Proclamation, conveyed by telegraph on receipt of it, were threefold. Only those guilty of heinous crimes against private persons were exempted from amnesty : hence men who had murdered their officers could claim pardon. The burden of proof was thrown on the officers of the Government. These again had no power reserved them to detain for inquiry such soldiers as might give themselves up.

Mr. Colvin at once pointed out that the Proclamation was a Hindustáni document addressed to Hindustáni soldiers. The words 'private persons' were expressed in the vernacular in terms which every native would at once understand. Resistance to public authority was distinguished from the commission of acts against the lives or persons of individuals. The latter were declared by the Proclamation to be unpardonable. The former alone would be condoned[1]. On the vernacular purport of

---

[1] The vernacular version is this : 'Siraf wuh log jo hangámah men fasád ke sarghanah wa sardár the, aur wuh, jinhon ne riyáya par kuch juram sangin kiye hon, albatta sazá pawenge.' This, by a Sepoy, would be read : 'Only those who in the disturbances have taken a chief and leading part in mutiny, and those who have committed any heinous crime against the people, will assuredly be punished.' Soldiers who had killed their officers fell directly under the first exception.

the Proclamation the Lieutenant-Governor could not
be gainsaid. There was no better authority in Calcutta, or out of it, on such a point. No one in the
Provinces, where Hindustáni is the vernacular, ever
misunderstood it. That is enough proof of its true
meaning, if it were possible that proof is still wanting. The version sent to Lord Canning, it will be
remembered, was but an English translation. It had
been drafted in the midst of 'a thousand distractions,'
Mr. Colvin said. The English translation was incor-
rect; but the vernacular text was the real issue, and
that offered no loophole to guilty Sepoys.

But what of the *onus probandi*, the absence of
any power of detention? Mr. Colvin must have felt
when he read those words, how little the Governor-
General could have realized what was passing at that
moment in Upper India. It was not a time when
men were trusting their lives to points of law, but
defending them at the point of the bayonet. No
Sepoy would have ventured to give himself up who
was not prepared to furnish proof and to face detention. Certainly, no guilty Sepoy would have risked
his neck on the chance of escaping through the verbal
meshes of a Proclamation. Such a fear could only
have found expression in a distant Council-Chamber,
uninformed as to local feeling. To those who were
in the midst of the mutinies, the idea was unimaginable.
There are times when an ounce of local knowledge
is worth a wagon-load of eminent capacity. Unfortunately, there was no one at hand to point out that

whatever danger might threaten us in 1857 the fear
of Sepoys availing themselves of legal flaws in State
documents was not worth one moment's attention.

Minor points were taken, in addition to these two,
in a letter dated May 29. That letter, it may be
hoped, was the work of subordinates. The tone is
so recriminatory that, when the relative position of
the two men at the moment is remembered, one is
loth to believe that Lord Canning saw it. It was
firstly objected in that letter that the Proclamation
dealt with the military discipline of the Bengal Army.
This was beyond the competence of the Lieutenant-
Governor. The Governor-General should have been
referred to before its issue. It was a strange moment
in which to write of the military discipline of the
Bengal Army. In a disciplinary sense the Bengal
Army was already a thing of the past. There was
a rabble at Delhi, and hurrying to Delhi, and a
wavering remnant still in its cantonments. A few
days later, on June 13, in the debate on what came
to be known as the Gagging Act, Lord Canning
himself spoke of 'the general disaffection of the
Bengal Army in the North-West Provinces.' What
remained of it, even in the end of May, was under no
military discipline or restraint other than such as it
chose to submit to. Mr. Colvin sought to detach any
who might listen to him, from that disbanded and
disordered host. He did not recall those whom he
addressed to the ranks, but dismissed them to their
homes. The measure adopted was not a disciplinary

measure, for there was no longer any power of maintaining discipline. Still less was it a military manifesto: for military authority was practically extinguished. It was a measure of public security.

But in any case, he was told, he should have wired for approval. A reply would have come, in ordinary course of twenty-four or thirty-six hours. Twice in the letter of May 29 does the expression 'ordinary course' occur. There was 'no necessity for any extreme haste.' When, in the name of wonder could such necessity arise? Many regiments had already revolted; others were momentarily expected to break from their ranks. A sudden act of mutiny was known to have caused the Proclamation. Even as it was penned, a detachment from one of the regiments in Agra itself was on the eve of revolt. When Sir John Lawrence [1] asked the Commander-in-Chief to issue, on his own responsibility, an order abolishing the new cartridges altogether, he added, 'time does not admit of a reference to the Governor-General.' Pressed, as he conceived, by time and circumstance, Mr. Colvin acted in the same spirit. The Governor-General's telegram of May 15 (page 182), and his instructions issued on July 31, enjoining clemency and ordering individual inquiry, prove that it was not Mr. Colvin's policy which was condemned but his meaning that was misunderstood. Men will differ as to the standard by which to decide in such a crisis; as to how far in similar circumstances a man should

---

[1] *Life of Lord Lawrence*, vol. ii. p. 23.

take authority on himself. But on this point all must agree, that if one standard is more inapplicable than another by which to judge of acts done under great pressure, it is the standard of 'ordinary course.'

The Proclamation remained without effect; the soldiery saw no authority but their own, and therefore no need of pardon. Neither to that, nor to the Proclamation in very similar terms, by which Lord Canning superseded it, did a single Sepoy respond. One result, and one only, was achieved. It was not in the designs of the Government in Calcutta, but especially in view of the state of affairs existing at Agra, it was none the less deplorable. At a moment when it was of the first importance to the State that its chief representative in the revolted Province should be upheld, if not by material, at least by moral force, the Governor-General publicly abandoned him. No explanation, no remonstrance, no appeal, could induce Lord Canning to reconsider his decision. From that hour the Lieutenant-Governor was aware that he must not rely—no matter what might be his difficulties, his dangers, or his local knowledge—on the support of the Governor-General.

Lord Canning disavowed Mr. Colvin's Proclamation ; Sir Henry Lawrence adopted it. In his *Mutinies in Oudh*, Mr. Gubbins writes (p. 43) :—

'A copy of the Proclamation issued by Mr. Colvin, the Lieutenant-Governor of Agra, promising immunity from punishment to all Sepoys not concerned in murderous attacks upon Europeans, now reached Lucknow. Sir Henry

Lawrence did not disapprove of it, and directed the Judicial Commissioner to prepare and cause to be issued a·notification throughout the Province of Oudh holding out promises of clemency not inferior to those promised by Mr. Colvin to all revolted Sepoys who should return to their duty. Mr. Colvin's Proclamation has been mercilessly condemned; and, if the condemnation so pronounced be just, it must be extended to the still more lenient Proclamation issued by Sir Henry Lawrence.'

Mr. Gubbins adds, 'We understood the meaning which they (the words 'private persons') were intended to convey.' So did all who could understand the language in which the paper was drafted, or who took the pains to have it interpreted.

Mr. Colvin's comments on it, written two months later, on July 23, to a brother, may close the matter :—

'We here understood the vast extent of the danger that was opening on us, and the sincere and thorough delusion that the mass of the Sepoys were in about the intentions of the Government. Regiments were beginning to give way all round. To prevent the fatal mischief spreading it seemed the wisest thing that could be done to mark that we desired to be just, and to offer the means of retreat to those not already desperately committed, and who had been betrayed into the rebel ranks by the insane apprehension about religion, or by the inability of getting away from them. That those who had taken a leading, or a deliberately malignant part in the revolt would ever seek to take advantage of the Notification we knew to be quite out of the question. The chance that seemed open through the Proclamation of escape called forth the heavy censure at many distant points. But we, who were behind the scene, and knew the real spirit of the revolt, could not entertain such a supposition. The attempt to separate the comparatively innocent, to appeal through them to the feelings of the Regiments yet in obedience, seemed in my deliberate opinion, and still seems, the right and useful thing to do at that time. The Proclamation was simply and briefly worded, that it might be understood by the soldiery for whom it was meant. If ever there was a chance of the kind, it was at first, and I tried to seize it.'

The last point on which something must be said is the conduct of affairs in Agra itself. Three lines of action presented themselves. The Lieutenant-Governor and all the Christian community might withdraw into the Fort and await events; or the women and children might be sent into the Fort; or the whole community might remain in their homes, subject to adequate precautions against surprise. By a section of Mr. Colvin's advisers, the second course was violently pressed upon him. He decided on adopting the last. For a moment, on May 13, when the position was in its first obscurity, he thought of sending the women and children into the Fort; but, on reflection, he refused. The Fort was unprovisioned, and in every respect unprepared. His military force was too small to be divided. There was no mutinous force at hand; therefore there was no pressing risk. It was his duty to show a resolute front. He had with him an English regiment, and could organize volunteers. His officers in their Districts were endeavouring to hold their posts. He would not set the example of seeking safety behind walls. He could ensure at least the

security of Head Quarters. On May 22 he wrote
to Lord Canning that he would decidedly oppose
himself to any proposal for throwing his European
force into the Fort, except in the last extremity. In
Mr. Drummond, the Magistrate of Agra, he had a strong
man on whom he could rely to keep order. He gave
him uncompromising support; leaving him free in
the choice of his instruments, and in the execution
of his measures. Throughout May and June order
was maintained by the police. In the last days
of June, from June 26 onwards, when it was known
that a hostile force was approaching, women and
children were sent into the Fort. By then it had
been provisioned and made ready. Between June
30 and July 4 the rest of the community followed.
On July 5 the affair of Sháhganj took place. The
British troops were repulsed and retired to the Fort.
When the police saw the British beaten, they threw
over all discipline and dispersed. It could not have
been anticipated that they would do otherwise. But
it was not till a strong body of successful mutineers
threatened Agra that the shelter of the Fort was
sought. The British community could then enter it
without dishonour, and remain in it without apprehension.

Incredible abuse was heaped on the Lieutenant-
Governor for adhering to his resolve. Those best
qualified to describe the storm which assailed him
have done so, in terms which must be quoted. But
the subject is not one on which any could wish to

linger. Among the many scenes of heroism and
courage presented to us in India during 1857, the
eye rests gladly elsewhere than on the community
sheltered in the Agra Fort. They were secure, provisioned, unmolested. But they were animated, unhappily, by a spirit of contention, by party animosity,
by unworthy jealousies. These led to discreditable
wranglings with which readers of narratives of the
scenes at Agra are familiar; and which among the
pages recording the conduct of our countrymen and
countrywomen elsewhere in India, remain an un-
pleasing blot.

At the first Council held on May 11, Mr. Raikes
found the Lieutenant-Governor

'already exposed to the rush of alarm, advice, suggestion,
exhortation, and threat which went on increasing for nearly
two months, till he was driven broken-hearted into the Fort.'

He went into the Fort for other reasons, which will
be explained ; not broken-hearted, but driven in by
the success of a rebel force.

'The flame of mutiny and rebellion was on every side, and
dissensions arose when unity above all things was required
to husband our remaining strength[1].'   .   .   .   .   .   .
I cannot look back without emotion on those troublous days.
Exhausted by want of sleep[2], worn with anxieties that few men

---

[1] Mr. E. A. Reade's *Narrative of Events at Agra, from May to September*,
1857. Printed, not published.

[2] His rest was almost hourly broken. He had been known to
pass forty-eight hours without opportunity of sleep. It was doubtless in some such moment of exhaustion that the interview took
place, described at p. 67 of his *Indian Mutiny*, by Mr. Thornhill.

could sustain, Mr. Colvin's gentleness, forbearance, patience, which I daily witnessed, were little appreciated by those who hailed down upon him their pettiness, ill-nature, and ignorance. I can only say that there are letters among his papers to which my reply would have been a file of soldiers or policemen to put the writers under keeping. Residing out of the vortex of party clamour, I did not know at the time its full extent and rancour.'

Similar scenes were occurring at Lucknow. 'In spite of Sir Henry's well-known wisdom and sagacity,' writes his biographer [1], 'the extremity of the crisis caused many people to forget themselves; and from many persons of whose obedience and support he might have had reasonable expectation, he received remonstrances against his line of policy.' On June 12 Sir Henry Lawrence wrote to Mr. Colvin that one of his principal officers had been almost insubordinately urgent on him to disband certain native troops. The fact is that in a great crisis, in which authority is paralysed and fresh incidents are hourly brought to notice, the most self-assertive, the alarmist, and the excitable secure a brief pre-eminence. Mr. Colvin met the storm in silence; with 'gentleness, forbearance, patience.' He had his way, and he let others have their say. He showed, because he felt, great indulgence to men who believed that his line of action was endangering the lives of their wives and children.

The rumours which he repeats regarding Mr. Colvin's health at that time, like much in his narrative, were idle gossip. See p. 196 of this Memoir.

[1] *Life of Sir H. Lawrence*, ii. 348.

He conceived that honour and duty alike compelled him to adhere to his policy. He judged, rightly, that in May and June there was no urgent cause for apprehension; and he carried his purpose to the end. Such success as attended it was afterwards claimed by others for themselves; on him centred the burden of every mishap. But it was his business to set to all an example of restraint and self-control. It was not a time for responsible Englishmen in India to be putting one another 'under a file of soldiers.' He never, even in his private letters, so much as mentioned the dissensions around him. As fortune would have it, men who could have helped him in his anxieties were not with him. His private Secretary, Lieutenant-Colonel Carmichael, of H.M.'s 32nd Regiment, was on leave in the Hills; and like Mr. Campbell, who was on his way from the Punjab in May to join him as Secretary to his Government, he could not reach him through the intervening anarchy. Among those around him were but few with whom he was on terms of any intimacy.

As early as May 14 Colonel Glasford, R.E., had been appointed Commandant of the Fort, and directions had been issued to lay in supplies and to organize its defence. The task of seeing to the necessary accommodation for refugees, should it become necessary at a later hour, was confided to Captain Nicholls. A month later, on June 14, Colonel Fraser, the Chief Engineer, reported (in a paper before the present writer) that the defences were 'sufficiently respectable.' The military command of the town and of the bridge of boats over the Jumna was adequate. So were the accommodation for servants, the sanitary arrangements, the accommodation for cattle, the water supply. ' Four months' provision for 2,500 Europeans and 1,500 natives will be completed in two days.' The number in the Fort, at a census taken on July 27, was 3,531 Europeans and Eurasians, and 2,314 natives. For the next fortnight the provisioning went on ; and when, after the fight at Sháhganj on July 5, the whole community had entered the Fort, at least six months' provisions had been laid in.

A Committee was nominated somewhere about June 20, consisting of Colonel Glasford, R.E., Captain Campbell, R.E., and Mr. Drummond, to regulate, among other points, the terms of the admission of private property, to accompany persons entering the Fort. Orders issued in accordance with these recommendations, which, from obvious considerations of space and sanitation, were framed with stringency. On June 26 these orders were relaxed, and discretion was left to Colonel Glasford. Overcrowding in the hot, damp season was apprehended ; space was limited. The Agra residents wished to bring all that they valued with them into the Fort ; this to the Committee and to the Lieutenant-Governor seemed inadmissible. Afterwards, when cholera broke out among the crowded refugees, the wisdom of the order became evident. But public records and private property were left behind and looted, and discontent deepened.

May and June had passed in these preparations.
On June 4 the current business of the Government,
such as it was, was distributed by the Lieutenant-
Governor between Mr. Harington, Mr. Reade, Mr.
Muir, and himself; Mr. Colvin reserving to himself,
says Mr. Reade, ' the Foreign Department and defence
of the station.' The loss of Rohilkhand, the massacres
at Jhánsi, intercepted communication with Cawnpur,
culminated in the outbreak at Gwalior, and the flight
of the residents to Agra on June 15. About this time
Sir Donald (then Captain) Stewart, starting on his
daring ride from Aligarh to Delhi, spent a few hours
in Agra. He found Mr. Colvin, he has told the writer,
among all his anxieties, calm, cool, and cheerful. So
the month passed ; disorder without : within, dissensions. On July 2, as a rebel force was approaching
directly by the road on which the Government House
lay, Mr. Colvin moved to the house of the General.
On July 3 he was threatened with apoplexy. For
twenty-four hours, like Sir Henry Lawrence, when
similarly struck down by ' worry, constant anxiety,
and his overtasked frame [1],' he gave over the guidance
of affairs to a Committee. On the 4th he was carried
into the Fort. On the 5th he resumed his charge.
So violent was the outcry in the excited community
now crowded into the Fort against Mr. Drummond,
whom they chose to hold responsible for the defection
of the Police and the loss of property, that it became

---

[1] *Life of Sir H. Lawrence,* ii. 341.

inevitable, in the interests of order, to relieve him temporarily of his charge.

Mr. Colvin continued to do what he could to collect and to forward intelligence ; and to communicate with the Governor-General, and others. His papers show that he wrote constantly, and at much length ; trusting to some letters at least passing safely through. But to the last the Calcutta Government could not refrain from reproaches. It seems to have been thought in Calcutta that Mr. Colvin could see from Agra to Benares in June and July 1857, as clearly as one glances from Government House across the Maidán ; or that a letter could be sent from Agra to Calcutta as surely as from Chauringhi to Serampur. 'A full despatch,' he wrote to Lord Canning on July 30, 'goes on my supposed neglect in getting intelligence and in sending communications. In that matter I am certainly guiltless ; and I trust that many of my letters will have been intermediately received.' Thrice only does he allude to his health ; once on August 6 to Lord Canning ; once, a week before his death, on September 2, to Sir John Lawrence ; on September 4, to Mr. Campbell. To Lord Canning he closes a letter with the words, ' My own health is, I fear, much shaken.' To Sir John Lawrence he writes, 'If you ask my disease, it is the utter powerlessness, with such rotten agency as we have, of doing for the present any good.' To Mr. Campbell he writes in terms similar to those used to Lord Canning. He has been blamed by an historian of the Mutinies

for watching every detail of public business. 'He
would have served his country better by sparing himself this labour, and leaving room in his mind for
larger views of State policy.' Here is a ship almost
in the power of mutineers. A few of the crew contend
with them. The captain, isolated against his will, with
the aid of a handful of men guards at least one strong-
hold against violence. He would be better employed,
says this critic, in entrusting defence to others, and in
leaving room in his mind for larger views of seaman-
ship and navigation. Such is the foolishness with
which men are assailed when that *turba Remi*, which
follows fortune, forsakes them.

The end drew near. On September 9, says Sir
George Campbell in his Memoirs, 'I have just received
a letter from Agra. Mr. Colvin is certainly the kindest
and most considerate of men.' This letter was dated
September 4.

'I thought you would be glad of the commission which
I have officially given you to prepare the outline of a scheme
for recasting the administration of the country in all
branches. This will be a fine field for maturing the results
of your North-West Provinces and Punjab experiences.
Whether I can co-operate with you as I would heartily desire
in the great work is more than I can say. My health is very
seriously shaken, and we may still have much to go through.'

These were probably the last words he ever dictated
(for latterly he could not write). He had not now
'much to go through.' The doctors had in vain
entreated him to give over his charge temporarily to

others. He had been told that unless he did so, he must succumb. But he believed it his duty to retain his trust, and he sank gradually under the burden. Exhaustion, sleeplessness, an overtaxed mind, combined with the strain of his position, the grief which he suffered from the loss of his charge, and the death of so many about him, prepared him for the assaults of disease. There was the sense of desertion by the Supreme Government; the burden of controversy with his countrymen. He seems to have foreseen his fate so far back as the close of July, though his frequent letters throughout August and up to September 4, show no sign of mental weakness. What that long effort cost him none will ever know. He bore for two months what he had to go through, in silence, making no complaint, carrying himself as became his high position. But on July 27, after a careful review of the state of affairs throughout Upper India, so far as it was known to him, he had written to Mr. Mangles, Chairman of the Court of Directors : 'I send my affectionate regards to all my old friends. I cannot shut my eyes to what is probably before me. If I have erred in any step, hard has been my position ; and you will bear lightly on my memory.' He perished, wrote one who was at Agra with him, because, in spite of the entreaties of his friends, he would persist in continuous mental labour, when his physical state demanded complete repose [1]. He gave up his life for his country.

---

[1] Raikes, *Revolt in the North-West Provinces of India*, p. 68.

said another, as much as if he had fallen, sword in
hand, on the battle-field [1].

His son Elliot was with him. Of the last sad days
passed in the marble enclosure, occupied by him on
that terrace of the 'Vine Garden' which overlooks
the turbid Jumna, little record is left which should be
published. He sank gradually, quietly. His thoughts
were with those by whom he had ever been held in
loving reverence. He was heard to murmur, in the
words of Virgil, that he must not hope to see his
own again. The end found him ready. He died, he
said to Dr. French (afterwards Bishop of Lahore), at
peace with all men. He had ever been a devout but
unassuming believer in the doctrines of Christianity.
In his last moments he turned with especial confidence
to the assurances of its great Apostle, in regard to the
promise of God, and to the hope therein centred, which
is 'an anchor of the soul, both sure and steadfast.'

In the first of the three Psalms which we read in
the morning service of the day on which he died,
Israel, straitly compassed by his enemies, appeals for
deliverance to Jehovah. He has become a byword
among the heathen. All the day long is he killed.
His confusion is daily before him. But before the
third Psalm has come to a close, Death has been
again swallowed up in victory. For the Strength of
Israel has not forsaken him. He has made wars to
cease. He has broken the bow. He has knapped the

---

[1] Sir James Colvile's Speech at a public meeting held in Calcutta,
1857.

spear in sunder. He has burned the chariots in the fire.

In the latter half of September success smiled again on the British arms in India. The tide of events in the North-West Provinces was turning, even as the Lieutenant-Governor was carried to his grave. He died on September 9. Had he lived but a few days longer he would have heard of the fall of Delhi. But though he had shared the confusion of his countrymen, he was not to join in their triumph. With the end of the rainy season, in the first days of October, Nature, in Upper India, relieved from the stress and languor of heat, smiles again with an abundant harvest, and receives into her keeping the seed of the coming spring crops. The cloud which had rested over the land cleared; the sun shone with a more temperate beam; there commenced that long era of repose, which still happily continues. Success was garnered, hope renewed. In that hour death removed him. Others entered into his labours, reaping where he had planted. Shortly after him the old order, too, passed away. The East India Company gave way to the Crown. The book of its chronicles was closed.

His services, like those of Mr. Thomason, his predecessor, had not been recognized by so-called honours. But to be one of the class to which Mr. Thomason and Mr. Colvin belong is in itself a rare distinction. It is because of such men that British rule is acceptable to the people of India. Their lives and their labours are built into the length and breadth of its

foundations.   Unrecognized, it may be, and little
honoured in England, their names are household words
in the greatest Province of her Empire. They illustrate
in their persons the best traditions of the service,
the worthiest ambition of the country to which they
belong.   For it is through such as they were that the
natives are convinced among much which is dark and
discouraging, of the goodwill and the honest purpose
of their alien and unseen rulers. The air is clearer
where they have passed. Their actions blossom in
the dust. Yet the legacy of their lives is to be found
in their character even more than in the tale of their
achievements.

When the news of Mr. Colvin's death reached Lord
Canning, he sat down, says Lady Canning[1], and wrote
the notification which ensues. The recurrence three
times in those few lines of the word 'high' betrays
the haste with which, among the pressure of the
writer's labours, it was composed. It indicates none
the less clearly, perhaps the more clearly, the idea
which, in connexion with Mr. Colvin, predominated
in the mind of the Governor-General.

'It is the melancholy duty of the Right Honourable the
Governor-General in Council to announce the death of the
Honourable John Russell Colvin, the Lieutenant-Governor·
of the North-West Provinces.

'Worn out by the unceasing anxieties and labours of his
charge, which placed him in the very front of the dangers by
which of late India has been threatened, health and strength

---

[1] *The Story of two Noble Lives*, vol. ii. p. 305.

gave way; and the Governor-General in Council has to
deplore with sincere grief the loss of one of the most distinguished amongst the servants of the East India Company.
The death of Mr. Colvin has occurred at a time when his ripe
experience, his high ability, and his untiring energy would
have been more than usually valuable to the State. But his
career did not close before he had won for himself a high
reputation in each of the various branches of administration
to which he was at different times attached ; nor until he
had been worthily selected to fill the highest post in Northern
India ; and he leaves a name which not friends alone, but all
who have been associated with him in the duties of Government, and all who may follow in his path, will delight to
honour.'

This Memoir may close with two brief extracts
showing the estimates formed of Mr. Colvin by men
who knew him in widely different spheres, but who
were not biased, as others who spoke or wrote of
him may have been, by much personal intimacy. Mr.
Ritchie, the Advocate-General in Calcutta, who had
known him as a Judge in the Sadr Court, said of him
at a public meeting held in his honour in the end
of 1857 :—

‘While no man's measures have in this country caused
greater difference of opinion, or excited louder remonstrance
or opposition, no doubt was ever cast upon the purity of his
motives, or the excellence of his character. As Secretary to
Lord Auckland, in fair weather and in foul—at first in
success and triumph, and afterwards in defeat and difficulty
and sorrow—as administrator of the Tenasserim Provinces—·
as the leading mind in that great Court of Appeal to which
such frequent allusion has been made—as Governor of the

North-Western Provinces in days of peace and prosperity—as virtually their dictator in the hours of darkness and distress which followed, and which are but now passing away, he supported or originated many measures which were most freely and warmly canvassed. No man more than he spurned the spurious popularity which seeks to catch the fleeting suffrages of the multitude; yet no man ever came out of so trying an ordeal with his personal honour more unsullied, with his personal character less assailed. When he died, he died lamented and respected by all; and by none more than by those by whom one of the last acts of his public life had been most strongly, and, as many of us think—for we would scorn to flatter even the dead—most justly opposed.' (The reference is to the Proclamation of May 25.) 'In him the loyal natives of this country, the Government and the Civil Service, have sustained a great and lasting loss; and among the many distinguished men whom that service has produced, though some may have surpassed him, in this or that element of distinction, no name will stand higher for unfailing constancy in the discharge of duty, for unswerving integrity and desire to do right, for the bright example which he set in the land, of a high-minded, upright, Christian English gentleman, pious but unbigotted, zealous but tolerant, firm but kind, just but merciful.'

Mr. Reade, whose narrative has been quoted, had known Mr. Colvin chiefly since the latter became Lieutenant-Governor. He writes of him thus in his narrative :—

'On September 9 he sank under the weight of anxieties and toil that can be hardly appreciated. Probably no public officer in our Indian annals was ever placed in a more trying conjuncture. The principle of the policy he maintained, of resolute defiance at the seat of Government, was indisputably sound ; but he erred in some respects in the choice of means, though he used the means employed with marvellous ability.'

Referring to his administration before Mutiny days he adds :—

' He had not the inestimable advantage of his eminent predecessor (Thomason), in that practical knowledge of the people, which can only be obtained by some years of close personal intercourse and minute acquaintance with their feelings, habits, peculiarities, and traditions ; and he did not in consequence avail himself of a strength which, judiciously managed, would have proved a powerful auxiliary. He pushed perhaps to an extreme, his theory that the cupola, not the pillars, should be the conspicuous feature of Government ; but he set an example of insurpassable devotion to the public service. His clear intellect had put aside his prepossessions in favour of a mechanical system of administration to which he had been long inured, but not suited to these Provinces (*sic*). He was ardently seeking the development of their resources, and the welfare of their communities. The State has never had a more devoted public servant, the people, a more earnest and liberal ruler.'

Where our dead fall in India, they lie. They are buried by her rivers, in her forests, among her mountains, on her roadsides. Lucknow, Delhi, Ghazipur, Cawnpur—a score of cities, claim their dust. In the Agra Fort, where Mr. Colvin rests, a monument was raised over his remains by the pious care of a successor. His tomb stands in conspicuous solitude before the deserted Audience Hall of the Emperor Akbar. As we linger by it, our thoughts recur to the past. We hear the waters rolling in upon the distant Scottish shore; the murmuring of pines on peaceful Simla hill-sides. The years glide on in pleasurable labour. Rest and retirement are in view. Of a sudden, in that fatal May, the land is smitten by a fiery blast of revolt and anarchy; and life is swallowed up in disaster. Endeavour, success, and disappointment have found in the grave their ending. But the spirit of man survives imperishable; and the purpose of predecessors, such as he was whose life has been traced in these pages, animates the best of those who yet labour in our Indian Empire.

The chief subjects which occupied public thought in India in Mr. Colvin's time exist, little modified, to this hour. Time has strengthened apprehensions as to the North-West frontier. But in 1894, as in 1838, there is conflict of opinion as to the measures necessary to defend it. Indian statesmen of the first rank, Lord Metcalfe and Lord Lawrence, are foremost on the one side; eminent English statesmen, Lord Palmerston, Lord Beaconsfield, on the other. One party hold that a policy of active defiance is inseparable from a policy of aggression, and point to 1838 and 1878; the other asserts that passive expectation, however completely forewarned and forearmed, must end in unquestionable defeat. There are some in England who think, with Lord Palmerston, that the defence of India is 'entirely an Indian question.' In India are many who, if this is to be so, regard the risks from internal discontent consequent on increasing taxation, as greater than those of invasion. But these are not pages in which the question can be discussed.

Progress through order is the maxim of Indian administration. To the superficial observer the disorder of 1857 may seem impossible of recurrence. Everywhere the eye rests now upon railways, telegraphs, schools, municipalities, district boards, newspapers, English education. It is what the eye does not rest upon, however, which in all organisms is vital. Fanaticism, bigotry, poverty in high places, the pride of ancestry, the pretensions of caste, love of change, lust of adventure, that Bacchic fury which blazes out so unaccountably in the East, slumber lightly beneath the sprinkling of Western soil. To these, British rule has added new elements of complication, fresh groupings of bodies, more active interchange of native opinion, wider combination, growing knowledge, the germs of strange hopes. The art of British government in India has hitherto been not to destroy, but to correct, Eastern methods of administration by applying to them the discipline of the Western mind. Now, it is the indisciplined Eastern mind which is to introduce into India Western methods of administration. The experiment will prove of interest, and, it is earnestly to be hoped, of value. But the lesson of 1857 must not be forgotten. Whatever may be hazarded with the educated minority, the real India is to be found only in the masses of her ignorant millions. To govern this real India

authority and justice should be in full view ; but in
reserve must be ample force. These are the only
methods which, under their own rulers, the masses
in that country have ever respected ; nor, even at
the desire of the British Government, will they readily
adopt any other.

INDEX

—+—

THE END.

CLARENDON PRESS, OXFORD

HISTORY OF INDIA

THE IMPERIAL GAZETTEER OF INDIA. New edition. To be completed in twenty-six volumes. 8vo. Subscription price, cloth, £5 net; morocco back, £6 6s. net. The four volumes of 'The Indian Empire' (I, III, IV are ready) separately 6s. net each, in cloth, or 7s. 6d. net with morocco back; the Atlas separately 15s. net in cloth, or 17s. 6d. net with morocco back. Subscriptions may be sent through any bookseller.

A BRIEF HISTORY OF THE INDIAN PEOPLES. By Sir W. W. HUNTER. Revised up to 1903 by W. H. HUTTON. Eighty-ninth thousand. 3s. 6d.

RULERS OF INDIA. Edited by Sir W. W. HUNTER. Crown 8vo. 2s. 6d. each.

BÁBAR. By S. LANE-POOLE.

AKBAR. By Colonel MALLESON.

ALBUQUERQUE. By H. MORSE STEPHENS.

AURANGZÍB. By S. LANE-POOLE.

MÁDHAVA RÁO SINDHIA. By H. G. KEENE.

LORD CLIVE. By Colonel MALLESON.

DUPLEIX. By Colonel MALLESON.

WARREN HASTINGS. By Captain L. J. TROTTER.

THE MARQUIS OF CORNWALLIS. By W. S. SETON-KARR.

HAIDAR ALÍ AND TIPÚ SULTÁN. By L. B. BOWRING.

THE MARQUIS WELLESLEY, K.G. By W. H. HUTTON.

MARQUESS OF HASTINGS. By Major ROSS-OF-BLADENS-BURG.

MOUNTSTUART ELPHINSTONE. By J. S. COTTON.

SIR THOMAS MUNRO. By J. BRADSHAW.

EARL AMHERST. By ANNE T. RITCHIE and R. EVANS.

LORD WILLIAM BENTINCK. By D. C. BOULGER.

THE EARL OF AUCKLAND. By Captain L. J. TROTTER.

VISCOUNT HARDINGE. By his son, VISCOUNT HARDINGE.

RANJIT SINGH. By Sir L. GRIFFIN.

THE MARQUIS OF DALHOUSIE. By Sir W. W. HUNTER.

RULERS OF INDIA (*continued*).

THE GOVERNMENT OF INDIA, being a digest of the Statute Law relating thereto; with historical introduction and illustrative documents. By Sir C. P. Ilbert. New edition, 1907. 10s. 6d. net.

THE EARLY HISTORY OF INDIA FROM 600 b.c. TO THE MUHAMMADAN CONQUEST, including the Invasion of Alexander the Great. By V. A. Smith. 8vo. With maps, plans, and other illustrations. 14s. net.

THE ENGLISH FACTORIES IN INDIA, 1618–1621. By W. Foster. 8vo. (Published under the patronage of His Majesty's Secretary of State for India in Council.) 12s. 6d. net.

WELLESLEY'S DESPATCHES, TREATIES, and other Papers relating to his Government of India. Selection edited by S. J. Owen. 8vo. £1 4s.

WELLINGTON'S DESPATCHES, TREATIES, and other Papers relating to India. Selection edited by S. J. Owen. 8vo. £1 4s.

HASTINGS AND THE ROHILLA WAR. By Sir J. Strachey. 8vo. 10s. 6d.

HENRY FROWDE

OXFORD UNIVERSITY PRESS

LONDON, NEW YORK AND TORONTO